"You Will Never Kiss Me,"

Clio said, finding her voice.

Jalal's hands stilled their motion. The heat was too much. She felt burned.

"Do you challenge me, Clio? When a woman challenges a man, she must beware. He may accept her challenge."

She had no idea why Jalal's words created such sudden torment in her, or what that torment was. Her whole body churned with feeling. She wished he would get away from her so she could breathe.

"Why doesn't it surprise me that you hear the word *no* as a challenge?" she asked defiantly.

His thumb tilted her chin, bringing her face closer to his full mouth, and her heart responded with nervous, quickened pulse. He smiled quizzically at her.

"But I have not heard the word *no*, Clio. Did you say it?"

Dear Reader,

Twenty years ago in May, the first Silhouette romance was published, and in 2000 we're celebrating our 20th anniversary all year long! Celebrate with us—and start with six powerful, passionate, provocative love stories from Silhouette Desire.

Elizabeth Bevarly offers a MAN OF THE MONTH so tempting that we decided to call it *Dr. Irresistible!* Enjoy this sexy tale about a single-mom nurse who enlists a handsome doctor to pose as her husband at her tenth high school reunion. The wonderful miniseries LONE STAR FAMILIES: THE LOGANS, by bestselling author Leanne Banks, continues with *Expecting His Child,* a sensual romance about a woman carrying the child of her family's nemesis after a stolen night of passion.

Ever-talented Cindy Gerard returns to Desire with *In His Loving Arms,* in which a pregnant widow is reunited with the man who's haunted her dreams for seven years. Sheikhs abound in Alexandra Sellers' *Sheikh's Honor,* a new addition to her dramatic miniseries SONS OF THE DESERT. The Desire theme promotion, THE BABY BANK, about women who find love unexpectedly when seeking sperm donors, continues with Metsy Hingle's *The Baby Bonus.* And newcomer Kathie DeNosky makes her Desire debut with *Did You Say Married?!,* in which the heroine wakes up in Vegas next to a sexy cowboy who turns out to be her newly wed husband.

What a lineup! So this May, for Mother's Day, why not treat your mom—and yourself—to all six of these highly sensual and emotional love stories from Silhouette Desire!

Enjoy!

Joan Marlow Golan

Joan Marlow Golan
Senior Editor, Silhouette Desire

Please address questions and book requests to:
Silhouette Reader Service
U.S.: 3010 Walden Ave., P.O. Box 1325, Buffalo, NY 14269
Canadian: P.O. Box 609, Fort Erie, Ont. L2A 5X3

Sheikh's Honor
ALEXANDRA SELLERS

Published by Silhouette Books
America's Publisher of Contemporary Romance

For my sister
Donna.
She knows why.

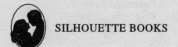 SILHOUETTE BOOKS

ISBN 0-373-76294-1

SHEIKH'S HONOR

This edition published by arrangement with Harlequin Books S.A.

® and TM are trademarks of Harlequin Books S.A., used under license.
Trademarks indicated with ® are registered in the United States Patent
and Trademark Office, the Canadian Trade Marks Office and in other
countries.

Visit Silhouette at www.eHarlequin.com

Printed in U.S.A.

Books by Alexandra Sellers

Silhouette Desire

#*Sheikh's Ransom* #1210
#*The Solitary Sheikh* #1217
#*Beloved Sheikh* #1221
Occupation: Casanova #1264
#*Sheikh's Temptation* #1274
#*Sheikh's Honor* #1294

#*Sons of the Desert*

Silhouette Yours Truly

A Nice Girl Like You
Not Without a Wife!
Shotgun Wedding
Occupation: Millionaire

Silhouette Intimate Moments

The Real Man #73
The Male Chauvinist #110
The Old Flame #154
The Best of Friends #348
The Man Next Door #406
A Gentleman and a Scholar #539
The Vagabond #579
Dearest Enemy #635
Roughneck #689
Bride of the Sheikh #771
Wife on Demand #833

ALEXANDRA SELLERS

is the author of over twenty-five novels and a feline language text published in 1997 and still selling.

Born and raised in Canada, Alexandra first came to London as a drama student. Now she lives near Hampstead Heath with her husband, Nick. They share housekeeping with Monsieur, who jumped through the window one day and announced, as cats do, that he was moving in.

What she would miss most on a desert island is shared laughter.

Readers can write to Alexandra at P.O. Box 9449, London NW3 2WH, U.K., England.

IT'S OUR 20th ANNIVERSARY!
We'll be celebrating all year,
Continuing with these fabulous titles,
On sale in May 2000.

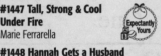

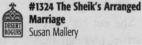

One

The green-and-white seaplane skimmed the tops of the trees, the drone of its engine loud as it headed for a landing on the next lake. Clio Blake, guiding the powerboat in hard jolts across the wake of a cruiser that had just emerged from the channel ahead of her, heard the sound first. As the plane roared over her head, she flicked a glance skyward and wished that her gaze held some magic that could make it disappear.

She did not want him here. He should not be coming. It wasn't right.

She cut her speed sharply and guided the boat into the narrow channel that led between two lakes, where signs posting the speed limit warned boaters of the danger of their wake eroding the shoreline. Some of the cottages were still boarded up, but most showed signs of having been opened for the season. At one cottage two men were working to take down the shutters, and Clio exchanged a wave with them as she passed.

Once through the channel and emerging into the larger lake, she reluctantly booted up her speed again and headed across the water towards the airline dock. The Twin Otter was already skimming along the surface, preparing to take off again.

So he was here. No hope left that something would prevent his arrival…. Seeing where her thoughts led, Clio grimaced self-consciously. Had she been unconsciously hoping for the plane to crash, then? Well, it only went to show how deep her opposition went.

But her parents had simply refused to listen. Her sister Zara had asked, and what Zara asked for, she still got. So Prince Jalal ibn Aziz ibn Daud ibn Hassan al Quraishi, the newly found nephew of the rulers of the Barakat Emirates, was here. For the entire summer.

She wondered if Prince Jalal was remembering their last meeting right now. *It is dangerous to call a man your enemy when you do not know his strength,* he had said then.

She had disdained to notice the threat, opening her eyes wide as if to say, *You and whose army?* But that had been a lie. She felt threatened in his presence, and who would not? He was the man who had taken her sister hostage to force his point on the princes of the Barakat Emirates.

Anything could have happened. They were all incredibly lucky that it had been resolved without bloodshed. It was enough to make him her enemy forever. That was what she had told him, that day at the fabulous, fairy-tale weddings, including Zara and Prince Rafi's. For her the celebrations had been deeply marred by the presence of such a man…even if, in the most outrageous turnaround of all time, he did have the title *prince* instead of *bandit* now.

It is dangerous to call a man your enemy when you do not know his strength.

Clio shivered. No doubt she would get to know his strengths—and weaknesses—over this coming, terrible summer. But one thing was certain—she would never forgive him for what he had done to them, the hell he had put them through, the risk he had run.

Whatever Jalal the bandit's strength was, he would never be anything to her but enemy.

Clio had always half-worshipped her older sister, though there were scarcely three years separating them. *Zary* was what Clio called her, right from her earliest speech. It was her own special nickname, and as a child she got ferociously jealous when anyone else tried to use the name.

Both girls took after their mother. Both had the black hair, the dark brown eyes, the beautiful bones...but Clio knew full well that she had always been a poor man's version of her perfect sister. Zara's hair fell in massed perfect curls, Clio's own hair was thick but dead straight. Zara was a fairy princess, with her exotically slanted eyes, delicate features, and her porcelain doll body. Clio's eyes were set straight under dark eyebrows that were wide, strong and level, giving her face a serious cast. Her eyelashes were not long, though lushly thick, and she had inherited their father's wide, full mouth rather than the cupid's bow that Zara had from their mother.

By the age of eleven Clio was already taller and bigger than her older sister. And in spite of being younger, she had begun to feel protective of Zara. She had always felt the urge to fight Zara's battles for her, even though Zara was perfectly capable of fighting her own. Half the time they weren't even battles Zara thought worth fighting.

Like now. Zara had forgiven and forgotten what Jalal had done to her. Clio knew *she* never could. It was Zara who had asked her family to have him for the summer, so that he could practise his spoken English before going on to a postgrad course somewhere…Clio, meanwhile, had been aghast. She had fought the idea with everything she had.

But she had lost the argument. And now here she was, picking up Jalal the bandit from his flight to the Ontario heartland, deep in the most beautiful part of cottage country, where the family lived and worked on the shore of Love Lake.

He was standing on the dock by two canvas holdalls. He had shaved off his neat beard since she last saw him. Perhaps he thought it would help him blend in, but if so, he hoped in vain. The set of his shoulders, the tilt of his chin as he took in his surroundings were indefinably different, set him apart from the men she knew.

He came out of his reverie when she hailed him, the boat sidling up to the concrete dock. The water level on the lakes was low this year, and he was above her.

"Clio!" he cried, ready to be friendly. So he was going to pretend to forget. Her jaw tightened. Well, she was not.

"Prince Jalal," she acknowledged with a brief, cool nod. "Can you jump in? Toss your bags down first."

He threw her one assessing look and then nodded, as if marking something to himself. She knew that the offer of friendship had been withdrawn, and was glad of it. It was good that he was so quick on the uptake. It would be best if they understood each other from the beginning.

"Thank you," he said, and picked up his bags to toss them, one after the other, into the well of the boat.

Then he stood for a moment, frowning down at the boat riding the swell of its own wake, as if trying to work out some obscure alien art. Clio realized with a jolt that he had probably never before performed the, to her, simple action of jumping into an unmoored boat.

And this was the man who was going to be so useful to her father at the marina! That was the argument her parents had made when she protested: with Jude gone off to the city, they needed someone...

"Take my hand," she said coolly, and, as she would with any green tourist, straightened and turned, keeping one hand steady on the wheel, while she reached her other up for his. "Step down onto the seat first."

She half expected him to refuse the help of a mere woman, but he bent over and reached for her hand. As his fingers brushed hers, Clio gasped, feeling as if his touch delivered an electric shock, and snatched her hand away.

Jalal tried to regain his balance on the dock and failed, but now he had lost his timing. The boat sank away from him just as his weight came down. He landed awkwardly on the seat with one foot, crashed down onto the floor of the boat with the other, skidded and involuntarily reached for Clio.

Her hands automatically clasped him, too, and then there they were—Jalal down on one knee before her, with his arms around her, his cheek pressed against the rich swell of her breasts, Clio with her arms wrapped around his sun-heated back and shoulders.

It was as if they were lovers. The heat of him burned her palms. She felt the brush of his breath at her throat.

For a moment the sun sparkled on the water with a brightness that hurt her eyes.

Clio stiffened. She was suddenly flooded with electric rage, her nerves buzzing and spitting like an overloaded circuit.

"Take your hands off me," she said.

Jalal straightened, glaring at her. He was seething with anger. She could feel the wave of it hit her.

"What is it you hope to prove?" he asked through his teeth.

Flushing under the impact of his gaze, Clio cried, "It wasn't deliberate! What do you think I am?"

He stood gazing at her. "I think you are a woman who sees things her own way. You choose to be my enemy, but you do not know what that means. If you try to make a fool of me again, you will learn what it means."

Nervous fear zinged through her at his words, at the look in his eyes. But she was damned if she would let him see it.

"I think I know, thank you." She had learned what it meant to be his enemy the day he had kidnapped Zara.

He shook his head once, in almost contemptuous denial, still eyeing her levelly. "If you knew, you would not play the games of a child."

"And what does *that* mean?"

"You are a woman, Clio. I am a man. When a woman sets herself to be the enemy of a man, there is always another reason than she imagines."

She opened her mouth, gasping at the implication. "Well, first prize for patriarchal, chauvinistic arrogance! And you from the modern, secular Barakat Emirates, too! You don't seem to have—"

He smiled and lifted his palm, and she broke off. "I am of the desert," he reminded her through his teeth.

"So I gathered!"

Three fingers gracefully folded down to his thumb, leaving the forefinger to admonish her. "In the desert a man will let a woman do much, because he is strong, and she is weak. He makes allowances."

Her blood seemed to be rushing through her brain and body at speeds never previously attained. "Of all the—!"

"In return, Clio, a woman never speaks to a man in such a tone of voice as this that you use to me. Women have sharp tongues, men have strong bodies. We respect each other by not using our strengths against the other."

"Are you threatening me?" she demanded.

"I only explain to you how men and women get along in a civilized country," he told her, and though now she was sure he was laughing at her, she couldn't stop the fury that buzzed in her.

"Well, that isn't how it is here!" she exploded. "And maybe you haven't noticed that, civilized or not, you aren't in the desert now!"

His lips were twitching. "I do know. We are going to hit the boat behind us, and this is a thing that would never happen in the desert."

Two

Clio whirled, diving instinctively for the wheel. She put the engine in gear, barely in time, and drew away from the small yacht moored at the next dock. What a racket there would have been from the anguished owner if she had collided with that expanse of perfectly polished whiteness!

It wasn't like her to forget herself like that when she was in charge of a boat. Clio had had water safety drummed into her with her earliest memories. It just showed what a negative effect *he* had on her.

But the sudden change of focus had the effect of calming her wild emotions. As she guided the boat over the sparkling lake, she understood that he had been deliberately baiting her, and was annoyed with herself for reacting so violently. She needed better control than that if she was going to get through the summer in one piece.

Jalal gazed at the scene around him. "This is the first

time I have seen such a landscape." He had an expression of such deep appreciation on his face that Clio had to resist softening. She loved this land. "It is beautiful."

She certainly would always think so. "But I guess you feel more at home in the desert," she suggested. She had not liked what she saw of the desert when she was in the Emirates. No wonder if an environment like that produced violent men.

"I am at home nowhere."

She stared at him. "Really? Why?"

He shook his head. "My grandfather Selim never meant me to follow in his own footsteps. When I was a little boy he told me always that something great was in store for me. I learned to feel that where I was born was not my true home. I belonged somewhere else, but I did not know where. Then my mother took me to the capital...."

"Zara told me that the palace organized your education from an early age," she said, interested in his story in spite of herself. He had a deep, pleasant voice. He engaged her interest against her will.

"Yes, but I did not know it then. Curious things happened, but I was too young to demand an explanation. Only when I approached university, and my mother gave me a list of courses to follow in my studies. Then some suspicion I had felt became clearer. I demanded to know who controlled my life, and why. But she would tell me nothing."

"And did you take the recommended degree?"

He laughed lightly at himself. He never told his story to strangers, and he did not understand why he was telling Clio. She had made it clear she was no friend.

"I never knew! I tore up the list, like a hothead. I said, now I am a man, I choose for myself!"

"And then?"

He shook his head, shrugging. "I graduated, I enlisted in the armed forces—and then again I felt the invisible hand of my protector. They put me into officer training. I rose more quickly than individual merit could deserve...still my mother was mute."

She could hear the memory of frustration in his voice.

"But you did eventually find out." Clio wondered if this story was designed to disarm her hostility by justifying his treatment of her sister. Well, let him hope. He would find out soon enough that what she said, she meant.

"Yes, I found out. It was on the day the princes came of age according to their father's will. The Kingdom of Barakat would be no more, and in its place there would be three Emirates. There was a great coronation ceremony, televised for all the country to see. Television sets were put in the squares of the villages—a spectacle for the people, to reassure them of the power, the mystery, the majesty of their new princes."

She was half-smiling without being aware of it, falling under his spell.

"I watched in my mother's house. Never will I forget the moment when the camera rested on the faces of the princes, one after the other, coming last to Prince Rafi.

"Of course I knew we were alike—whenever his picture was in the paper everyone who knew me commented. But what is a photograph? True resemblance requires more than the face. That day...that day I saw Prince Rafi move, and speak, and smile, as if...as if I looked in a mirror instead of a television set."

She murmured something.

"And then it fell into place. The mystery of my life— I knew it had some connection with my resemblance to

Prince Rafi. I knew that the old man I had called my father was not my father.

"'Who am I?' I cried to my mother, trembling, jumping to my feet. 'Who is Prince Rafi to me?'"

"Did she tell you?"

He nodded. "My mother could no longer refuse, in spite of the shame of what she confessed. She was disappointed that the great future that they had promised for me for so many years had not arrived on this momentous day. 'He is your uncle,' she told me. 'The half brother of your father, the great Prince Aziz. You could be standing there today instead of them.'"

Jalal paused, a man hovering between present and past. "Of course I knew—every citizen knew—who Prince Aziz was, although it was over twenty-five years since he and his brother had so tragically died. Singers sang the song of King Daud's great heartbreak."

His eyes rested on her, but he hardly saw her. He was looking at the past.

"And this noble prince, this hero dead so young…was my father."

Clio breathed deeply. She had been holding her breath without knowing it. "What a terrible shock it must have been."

It would be something, a discovery like that. In a young man it might motivate…seeing where her thoughts were leading her, Clio mentally braked.

He nodded. "I was a lost man. As if I stood alone in a desert after a sandstorm. Every familiar landmark obliterated. All that I had known and believed about myself was false. I was someone else—the illegitimate son of a dead prince, grandson of the old king…how could this be? Why had I not been told?"

"What a terrible shock it must have been."

"A shock, yes. But very soon I felt a great rage. If they did not wish to recognize me because of the illegitimacy of my birth, why had they taken me from my ordinary life, for what had they educated me…? Why had I never met my grandfather, the king, and my grandmother, his most beloved wife, in all those years when my future was being directed—and to what purpose was it all? My grandfather was dead, and I was left with no explanation of anything."

He paused. The boat sped over the lake, and he blinked at the sun dancing off the water.

"What did you do?"

He glanced towards her, then back to the past again. "I made approaches to these new princes, my uncles. I demanded to know what my grandfather's plans for me had been."

"And they didn't tell you?"

He shook his head. "Nothing. They would not speak to their own nephew. I had been taken from my mother's home, but those who had done this thing would not let me enter my father's."

He turned to gaze intently at her. "Was this not injustice? Was I not right to be angered?"

"Zara told me they never knew. Your uncles, Rafi and Omar and Karim—they didn't know who you were. Isn't that right?"

"It is true that they themselves had never been told. They said afterwards that my letters, even, did not make the point clear. They thought me only a bandit. But someone had known, from the beginning. My grandfather himself…but he had made no provision for me in his will. No mention."

"Isn't that kind of weird?" It struck her as the least credible part of the whole equation.

His eyes searched her face with uncomfortable intensity.

"You would say that my uncles knew the truth, and only pretended ignorance until they were forced to admit it? Do you know this? Has your sister said something?"

She shook her head, not trusting the feelings of empathy that his story was—probably deliberately—stirring in her.

"No, I don't know any more than you've told me. It's just very hard for me to accept that a woman wouldn't insist on meeting her only grandchild, the son of her own dead son."

His face grew shadowed. "Perhaps—perhaps my illegitimate birth was too great a stain."

"And so they never even met you?" Clio tried to put herself in such a position, and failed. She herself would move heaven and earth to have her grandchild near her, part of the family, whatever sin of love his parents had committed.

"Nothing. Not even a letter to be given to me after their death."

No wonder he felt at home nowhere.

He was silent as they skimmed across the endless stretch of water, that seemed as vast as any desert.

"What did you do when your uncles refused your requests?"

He had made his way back to his "home," the desert of his childhood. But the bonds had been severed.

"The desert could never be home to me. The tribe—so ignorant, living in another century, afraid of everything new—could not be my family." So his determination to force his real family to recognize him grew. He had collected followers to his standard—and eventually...he had taken a hostage.

"And the rest you know," he said, in an ironic tone.

"The rest I know," she agreed. "And now your life has changed all over again. Thanks to Zara, you've proven your bloodline, you have your father's titles and property…and you're so trusted by your uncles they've made you Grand Vizier and now you're on a mission to—"

His head snapped around, and if his dark eyes had searched her before, they now raked her ruthlessly.

"Mission? Who has told you I had a mission?"

She returned his look with surprise. "I thought the reason you were coming here was to get a better command of English so you could study political science or whatever at Harvard in the autumn. I thought a summer with the rowdy Blake family was supposed to be the perfect way to do it."

The guarded look slowly left his eyes. "Yes," he said. "It is true."

Clio turned back to the water ahead of her, her mind buzzing with speculation. What on earth was that about? Did it mean he wasn't really here to learn English at all? That it was some kind of blind? But for what? What other reason could Prince Jalal possibly have for coming here to the middle of nowhere?

Three

Jalal stood and moved towards the stern, gazing around him as they passed into yet another lake. He lifted both arms, stretching out his hands in powerful adoration. "It is magnificent! So much water!" He breathed deeply. "Smell the freshness of the water! This water is not salt! Is it?"

A loud horn startled her, and Clio whirled to discover that she had turned onto a collision course with another boat. She waved an apology to the indignant pilot as she hastily and not very gracefully adjusted her course. Jalal half lost his balance and recovered.

"Dammit, don't distract me when I'm driving!" she cried. She had been staring over her shoulder at him. He had a huge physical charisma, but she would get over that. "No, of course it's not salt," she said when the danger was past. "All Canada's lakes are freshwater."

"*Barakallah!* It is a miracle. And you drink this water!'' He spoke it as a fact, but still he looked for confirmation from her.

''Yes, we drink it.'' She smiled, and then, realizing how much she had already let her guard down with him, steeled her heart against the tug she felt. ''For now. It may end up polluted in the future, like everything else.''

But his joy would admit no contaminants. ''It must be protected from pollution,'' he said, as though he himself might fix this by princely decree. ''This must not be allowed, to destroy such rich bounty.''

''Yes, really,'' Clio agreed dryly.

''Why do they pollute such beauty?''

''Because it is cheaper to dump than to treat waste.''

Prince Jalal nodded, taking it in. Was it his grandmother's blood in him that so called to this place?

''My mother's mother was raised in a country of lakes and forests.'' He spoke almost absently, as if to himself, and he blinked when she responded.

''Really? How did she happen to marry a desert bandit, then?''

''On a journey across the desert, she was abducted by my grandfather, Selim. She spent the rest of her life in the desert, but she never forgot her beloved land of lakes.''

The result of that union had been only one daughter, his mother. Desert-born Nusaybah had heard many longing tales of her mother's homeland as a child, and later she had passed them on to her son. She had also passed on the information that his grandmother was a princess in her own country.

That had seemed unlikely, until the DNA tests showed that he was more closely related to Prince Rafi than to Rafi's two half brothers. Then a search of the family tree showed that Rafi's mother, the Princess Nargis, was the daughter of a prince whose sister had been abducted and never spoken of again.

For centuries the family had spent every summer in the highlands, just as Jalal's grandmother had always said. So it was deep in his blood, the longing for lake and forest, though he had not felt its force until he saw these sights.

Clio frowned. "She spent the rest of her life in the desert? She was never rescued?"

He shook his head. "In those days no one would have troubled. She had no choice but to marry her abductor."

"You mean her family knew where she was but *left* her there?"

"I cannot say what they knew, only what was the tradition. A woman captured by a man in this way...her family would have ignored her existence from that moment."

She threw a look over her shoulder at him. "And you accept that?" she demanded incredulously.

"There is nothing for me to reject, Clio. It was finished, many years ago. I am here because of it. My mother Nusaybah was the child of that union. What shall I say? *Maktoub.* It is written."

"So that's in your blood too, is it—abducting women? I suppose that makes it all right! Were you expecting my family and Prince Rafi to leave my sister Zara to her fate?"

He shook his head impatiently, but did not reply.

"But no," she supplied for him. "That wouldn't have served your purpose! You knew Rafi had to get her back—world opinion would dictate that. You probably thought he'd refuse to marry her, but that wouldn't have bothered you. If you spoiled their love, it would be just their bad luck, wouldn't it? So long as you got what you wanted."

"I did not reason in this way," he said levelly. "I believed that he would want her back and would make her his wife when I released her unharmed."

She had succeeded in talking herself into deep anger. She could not trust herself to make an answer.

So he was a chip off the old block. Did her parents know this about Jalal's genes? But she didn't suppose it would have made any difference. If they weren't concerned about what *he* had done to Zara, they'd hardly worry about what his grandfather had done to a nameless princess fifty years ago.

A few minutes later they arrived at a large, rambling brick house. It was on the shore of a very pretty lake, smaller than those they had crossed to get here. There were tree-covered hills rising high around one end of the lake, as if some spirit brooded protectively over the water. Fewer houses dotted the shore.

As they approached their destination, he saw a marina clustered with boats on one side, and a pretty painted sign high on one wall of the house that advertised homemade ice cream, a crafts shop and an art gallery.

Clio guided the powerboat in, cut the engine and expertly brought it up beside the dock. Meanwhile, the door of the house exploded outward, and at least half a dozen children of all ages, four dogs and a couple of cats erupted into the morning to cries of "Is he here? Did the prince come? What does he look like?" and loud excited barks.

Everybody raced down to the dock, except for the cats, who dashed up the trunk of a large, leafy tree that overhung the water so picturesquely he felt he was in some dream, and clung there indignantly, staring at the scene.

"Calm down, yes, he's here and he doesn't want to be deafened on day one! Here, Jonah, grab this!" Clio commanded lazily, tossing the mooring rope as a tall boy ran to the bow. The dock beside the boat was stuffed with children and canines, all gaping at him and all more or less panting with excitement.

"Is that him? Is that the prince?" In the babble he could pick out some sentences, but most of what they were saying was lost, as always when too many people talked at once in English.

"He isn't weawing a cwown!" one tiny creature cried piercingly, her woebegone eyes locking onto Jalal's with heartfelt grief.

Clio and Jalal exchanged glances. She resisted the impulse to laugh with him.

"The natives are restless," he observed.

Then she did laugh; she couldn't help it.

"I should have realized what the result of an hour's wait would be. They were excited enough about you when I left. Out of the way, everybody! Prince Jalal wants to get onto the dock. He isn't ready to go swimming yet!"

One of the dogs was, however, and leapt off into the water with a loud splash.

Meanwhile, Jalal braved the natives to step onto the dock.

"Are you Prince Jalal?" "Are you a real prince?" "Where's—"

"Cool it!" Clio cried beside him. "What did I tell you?" Getting a general reduction in the babel, she reeled off their names. "Rosalie, Benjamin, Sandor, Alissa, Jonah, Jeremiah, Arwen and Donnelly. Everybody, this is Prince Jalal."

"Welcome to Canada, Your Highness," said several voices in ragged unison, and the welcome was echoed as the laggards caught up. And then Jalal watched transfixed as, to his utter astonishment, they all bowed. From the waist.

He couldn't restrain the bursting laughter that rose up in him. Their heads tilted at him in surprise. "Thank you!" he exclaimed, when he could speak. "I am very glad to be here. But I am not used to such bowing, or this name, Your High-ness!"

"But Clio said people have to bow to princes."

"Clio said we had to call you Your Highness."

He flicked her a glance, as if to an awkward child. She returned the look impassively, then bent to the task of tying the stern rope.

"Clio did not know. She thought I was a tall man," he said, his lips twitching, and she thought, *He thinks I'm not a worthy enemy, but he'll find out.*

"You *are* tall. You're as tall as Daddy."

"What will we call you, then?"

"Why not call me—Jalal? That is my name, and it will make me feel very welcome if you use it. Then I will think we are friends. Shall we be friends?"

"Oh, yeah!" "Cool." "Sure."

"I'm your fwiend, Jalal," said Donnelly confidingly, reaching up to put her hand in his. She had clearly taken one of her instant likes to him.

His smile down at the child would have melted Clio on the spot, if she hadn't steeled herself.

"Don't people bow to princes?" Arwen asked, her head cocked on one side.

"Yes, people bow to princes, unless," he said, raising a forefinger, "unless they are given special dispensation. And since we are going to be friends, I give you all special dispensation."

"But you are a real pwince, aren't you?" It was the

little curly-haired darling again. Jalal squatted down to face her.

"My father was the son of a king. My mother's mother was a princess. Am I a prince?"

Her eyes were wide. "Ye-es," she said, half asking, half telling. She looked around her, then up at that fount of wisdom, seventeen-year-old Benjamin.

"Of course he's a prince, Donnelly, that's how you get to be a prince—your father was one," Ben said knowledgeably.

"But you don't have a cwown," she reminded Jalal. "You don't look like the picture."

"Do you have a picture of a prince?" he asked.

Donnelly nodded mutely. Jalal lifted his arm, and she snuggled in against him as confidingly as a kitten. "Well, I have a crown, my father's crown, but princes don't go swimming in crowns, do they?"

"They don't?" Donnelly sounded disappointed, as if she had been hoping to see just that sight.

"No." Jalal, smiling, shook his head firmly. All the children had fallen silent, listening to him, almost entranced. "Do you wear your swimsuit to school?"

Donnelly, who did not go to school, gazed at him wide-eyed, and shook her head with mute solemnity.

"Princes only wear crowns in their palaces. There is no palace here. So I left my crown at home."

"Ohhhh."

"But one day, I hope you'll come and visit me in my home, and then I'll show you my crown."

"Oh, neat! Can I come, too?" "Do you have a palace?" "Can I come, can I come?" "Is your home in the desert?" "Is it an Arab's tent or is it a real palace?" "Do you have camels, Jalal?" "What's it like in the desert?" "Were you a bandit before you were a prince, Jalal?"

And then somehow, in a circle of fascinated children, the two oldest boys carrying his cases, Jalal was being led up to the house, into the kitchen. Clio stood on the dock watching the progress of the little party.

No doubt she should have realized that a man capable of drawing as many followers to his cause as Jalal was said to have had would have powerful charisma. She didn't like the way they were all falling all over him, but there wasn't much she could do about it.

Not right now, anyway.

Four

"Uncle Brandon dropped the guys back and went out again. He said not to save lunch for him," Rosalie reported, when Clio entered the kitchen.

That wasn't unusual in the run-up to the season. He had probably had to go for more creosote or something, and would grab a hamburger in the plaza. But Clio would rather her father had been here to meet Jalal.

"You've got lunch going already?" she asked, sniffing the air. "That's terrific, Rosalie."

Whenever her mother was absent on one of her buying trips among the First Nation artists she represented in the gallery, as she was this week, Clio was in charge. This year Rosalie, who had arrived in tears shortly after Christmas declaring that she hated her new stepmother, was proving to be a big help in filling the gap left by Romany. Romany was on a visit to Zara and Rafi.

"What's cooking?"

Rosalie told her, and the two cousins began to organize the meal.

Jalal was at the table, surrounded by kids. Everyone had something to show him, a question to ask....

"You have to choose a plaque." Sandor was informing him gravely about one of the house rituals. Sandor himself had moved in only a month ago, so he knew all about it. "It's for the duty roster."

They had spread the available plaques out in front of him, and Jalal was considering his choice, though she doubted if he was making sense of the garbled explanation he heard, from several sources.

"Okay, everybody, the table needs to be set!" Clio announced, not sorry to break up the group. "Sorry, your fan club has work to do," she added dryly to Jalal.

Jalal nodded impassively, recognizing the jealousy in that.

"He has to choose a plaque first!" someone exclaimed indignantly, and of course Clio had to give in.

"What is Clio's plaque?" Jalal asked, as he browsed among the little squares of plastic, each with a different image on it, that were reserved for the use of visitors. For the length of his stay, this plaque would represent him.

"Clio's the pussycat," Donnelly articulated carefully. She pointed to the duty roster on the wall. "The black-and-white one. I'm the butterfly."

"All right. I will take this one," Jalal said, choosing a plaque with his finger and drawing it out of the spread.

"The tiger!" they chorused.

"He's a very *wild* tiger!" Donnelly informed him impressively.

Clio tried, but she could not keep her eyes away.

He was watching her gravely, and something unspoken

passed between them. Something that made her deeply nervous.

"Right, then! He's chosen a plaque! Let's clear the table!" she cried, and the children all moved to their usual mealtime tasks.

"And I," Jalal said. "What shall I do to assist?"

She had been hoping that he would expect to be served. She had been anticipating telling him that in this kitchen, everyone did their share, male and female, bandit and *nouveau* prince alike. She flicked him a glance, and saw that he was watching her face as if he could read her thoughts there. He gave her an ironically amused look, and she blushed.

"You can help me, Jalal," an adoring voice said. "I have to fold the serviettes."

One of the boys snorted. "Princes don't fold serviettes, Donnelly!" he began, but Jalal held up a hand.

"No job worth doing is beneath any man." And it infuriated Clio even more to see Ben nodding in respectful agreement, as if he had just learned something profound.

Jalal smiled down at Donnelly. "I would like very much to help you," he said. "Will you teach me to fold them just right?"

It wasn't often that Donnelly got to pass on her wisdom to anyone; she was usually on the receiving end. At Jalal's words, her chest expanded with a delighted intake of air.

"It's very important to match the edges!" she informed him.

A few minutes later they all sat down, amid the usual mealtime babble. When their parents were at the table, a certain amount of order was imposed, keeping it, as their father Brandon said, to a dull roar. But when Clio was in charge, she didn't usually bother. It didn't hurt anyone if once in a while bedlam reigned.

But the first time someone said, "Is that true, Jalal?" and the prince replied quietly, "I am sorry, I didn't understand. When everyone talks at the same time, I can't follow," a respectful hush fell on them.

After that, it was, "Shhh! Jalal can't follow!" when anyone tried to interrupt the current speaker.

Then lunch was over, and there was the usual competition to be first to get their plates into the dishwasher. Donnelly explained the task to Jalal, and again he performed it without apparently feeling that it was any assault on his masculinity or his princely status.

Clio was almost certain that he was doing all this just to spike her guns, because he had guessed that she was waiting to tell him how unimportant his princely status was here in the democratic confines of the Blake family, or to explain that male superiority had been superseded in the West. She was even more convinced of it when, straightening from having set his utensils in just the right place under Donnelly's tutelage, he threw her another of those glances.

"Round one to you," she bit out, feeling driven.

"Only round one? I have counted three," he observed mildly. "How many before we stop the match, Clio?"

The match went on, under cover of surface friendliness, for several days. Brandon showed Jalal the ropes at the marina for a couple of days, and on the following day Jalal and Ben started creosoting the marina dock while Jeremiah went with Brandon to work on one of the cottages, taking their lunch with them. Teaching at the high school had stopped, and the next three weeks was exams, but the younger children were still at school full-time.

It was a beautiful day, and when they broke at lunch the first coat was done.

"That's the fastest I've ever seen the first coat go on," Ben said. "You really know how to swing a brush."

The youthful admiration in his tone made Clio grit her teeth.

"I've had a lot of practice," Jalal said.

"Paint the palace a lot, do you?" Clio interjected.

Jalal gazed at her for a long moment, as if he was bored with her childish taunts.

"We've got another hour till the second coat can go on," Ben said. "Want to take a boat out? I could show you around."

"Thank you, Ben, another day. Just now, I would like to talk alone with your sister Clio."

The hair stood up on the back of her neck, but there was nothing she could say. Within a couple of minutes, she found herself alone with him in the big friendly kitchen. Tense, and angry because she was, Clio determinedly started her usual tasks.

"You dislike me very much, Clio," Jalal said. "Tell me why."

Taken aback by his directness, she shook her head and bent to scoop some dishwashing powder into the dishwasher.

He caught her arm, forcing her to straighten, and the touch shivered all through her. She did not want this. She was not at all prepared to start defending her attitude to him. And he had no right to demand it.

"I thought you weren't allowed to touch a woman not related to you," she said coldly, staring down at where his hand clasped her bare arm, just above the elbow. She felt under threat. She did not want to have this conversation.

He ignored her comment. "Tell me," he said. "I want to know why you alone are unwilling to be my friend."

She wrenched her arm out of his grasp, using far more effort than was necessary for such a light hold, and staggered.

"I told you at the wedding. We will never be friends."

"Why not?"

She was silent.

"Your sister has forgiven what I did. Your parents, too. Why cannot you?"

She turned her back on him deliberately, closed the dishwasher and set it going. He was silent, too, behind her, and her nerves didn't seem up to the strain. Her skin shivered with awareness of him.

"Do you believe it impossible that your sister took no hurt while she was my hostage? Do you suspect me of hurting her, or allowing her to be hurt?" he asked, finally.

She was silent. Was that what she feared? She hardly knew. All she knew was that Jalal was a threat, and she wished he had never come.

"Look at me, Clio."

His voice was seductive, almost hypnotic, though he did not seem to be doing that deliberately. Feeling driven, she turned to face him. He was too close. She thought dimly, *Middle Eastern people have a smaller body territory or something—they always stand too close for Westerners' comfort.* Her heart kicked uncomfortably.

"Can you imagine that Princess Zara would have encouraged me to come here, into the home of her own family, if such a dreadful thing had happened?"

"If she was pretending to herself it hadn't happened, she might," she felt driven to point out. It wasn't that she believed it, necessarily, but it was possible. He had to see that.

He stared at her, honestly startled. "Pretending to herself? How could a woman pretend such a thing? Why would she?''

Clio felt anxiety creeping up in her. "It does happen, you know! Women take the blame on themselves, or they don't want to face what happened to them! Denial does happen!''

He was silent, watching her. Then he said softly, "Does it, Clio? Are you sure?''

"If you understood anything about psychology you wouldn't have to ask.''

"Do you deny something? Has someone hurt you, so that it is easier to imagine I hurt your sister than to accept what happened to yourself?'' he asked, proving that he understood more than somewhat about psychology.

She gasped in indignant fury and clenched her fists. Never had she so wanted to hit someone. But she looked at Jalal and saw the warning in his eyes. Gentle as he was with the children, his look warned her that he would not be gentle with her if she attacked him.

"Nothing has ever happened to me!'' she exploded, her rage escaping in words. "Let's get one thing straight, Jalal—whatever did or did not happen in your camp, we're enemies, and it's because of what you yourself did.''

He shook his head in flat contradiction. "We are not enemies. That is not what is between us,'' he said softly.

Five

Clio opened her mouth soundlessly as shivers like a flood ran over her body.

"You make your sister an excuse to avoid what frightens you. That is all, is it not?"

He stepped closer, and she backed up against the counter. In the pit of her stomach a hard ball of fire suddenly revealed itself.

"I am not afraid!" she protested hotly.

"Good," he whispered, and when she lifted a hand in protest his hand wrapped her wrist. Every nerve leapt at the touch. Fury seemed to come from nowhere and whip against her like wild wind.

Slowly he bent closer. He was going to kiss her.

She couldn't allow it. She wanted to hit him. Something like a scream was in her throat and she wanted desperately to beat him off. But she couldn't seem to work her muscles.

"Do you always just do what you want without asking?" she demanded.

"I want to kiss you," he murmured thoughtfully, his mouth only inches from her own. "In this country, do men ask permission for such a thing?"

She tried to swallow. "Yes," she said defiantly. Her mouth felt as dry as the desert he came from, where the rules between men and women were so different. She wanted to push him away, to get to a place where the air was clear. But the unfamiliar lassitude would not let her go.

"Then they understand nothing." He drew closer, and she felt the heat of his arm encircle her back, his firm hand at her waist. His breath touched her cheek as his eyes challenged hers. She felt the look deep inside her, stirring the depths of her self.

He stroked the skin that she had so foolishly left bare between her short top and low-cut shorts. Sensation skittered down her body to her toes. Under the thin top, her breasts shivered.

Suddenly she was angry with *herself*. This was the man she had sworn only days ago would be always her enemy!

"What do men do in the desert?" she demanded cynically. "Grab whatever they see? Well, of course they do!" she told herself brightly. "You proved—"

"In the desert we first make sure that a woman longs for the kiss, and then we kiss her without asking."

The sheer male arrogance of such a statement caused angry fire to leap in her chest and abdomen. She clamped her teeth together, because she could hardly prevent herself from shouting at him that he was an arrogant barbarian. But he had warned her....

His hand was moving against her spine. His other hand touched her neck, and his thumb traced her jawline.

Her mouth felt swollen—not that she wanted any kiss from him! But he was as mesmerizing as a snake, he really was. She flicked her eyes up to his.

The naked desire she saw there shook her to the core. She had thought him attracted, but not as powerfully as this! He looked at her like a starving man. Clio's heart tripped into an unsteady rhythm. Feeling she didn't recognize roared through her.

"Then you will never kiss me," she said, finding her voice.

His hands stilled their motion. The heat was too much. She felt burned.

"Do you challenge me, Clio? When a woman challenges a man, she must beware. He may accept her challenge."

She had no idea why his words created such sudden torment in her, or what that torment was. Her whole body churned with feeling. She felt faint, almost sick. She wished he would get away from her, so she could breathe.

"Why doesn't it surprise me that you hear the word *no* as a challenge?" she asked defiantly.

His thumb tilted her chin, bringing her face closer to his full mouth, and her heart responded with nervous, quickened pulse. He smiled quizzically at her.

"But I have not heard the word *no,* Clio. Did you say it?"

Bee-bee-bee, bee-bee-bee.

They were both jolted by the high, piercing sound. Jalal frowned and looked around, and Clio tried to gather her wits.

"Is it a fire alarm?" he asked.

She finally identified the noise. "Oh, my God, it's an

intruder alarm!'' Clio cried, and as he released her she ran to the monitor panel above her father's desk in an alcove. A dozen lights glowed steady; one was flashing its urgent beacon. She bent down to read the tag.

''Solitaire!'' she breathed. ''It can't be Dad, he wasn't going there today.''

He watched as she opened a small cupboard and snatched up a set of keys, then stood back out of her way as she whirled and lightly ran to the screen door of the kitchen and opened it.

''Ben!'' she called.

Jalal followed her as she ran along the wooden porch and down onto the dock. When she reached the boat, he was right behind her. She quickly untied the stern rope, and when Jalal bent to the bow, Clio clambered aboard and started the motor. Meanwhile Rosalie and Donnelly raced towards the dock from further along the beach.

''The intruder alarm has gone off at Solitaire! It's probably a raccoon!'' she cried, as Jalal came aboard with more grace and expertise than his first effort. Clio swung the boat in a wide arc, and as they passed the end of the dock, she continued to Ben and Rosalie, ''You'd better call Dad! Tell him I'm on my way there and I'll call him if there's a problem.''

Rosalie stood holding Donnelly's hand, and all three were nodding. ''Be careful!'' And then Clio booted up the motor and the boat obediently climbed up out of the waves and planed across the surface at top speed.

''What is Solitaire?'' Jalal asked, settling beside her.

She blinked and seemed to see him for the first time. ''Oh, hi!'' she said. It had seemed so natural for Jalal to be there that it was only now she actively registered his presence.

"One of the rental cottages," she said. "It's kind of isolated."

He knew the family owned and rented cottages on the lakes. He had visited a couple with Brandon, doing repairs. "Will your father meet us there?"

Clio shrugged. "He might not bother unless I call to say it's something really bad. It depends where he is, I guess. Ben will tell him you're with me."

"What weapons are on this boat?"

Clio blinked. "What, you mean like a shotgun?" She shook her head. "Nothing that you could call a weapon. We aren't going to kill the raccoon, just open the door and scare him out. The point is to get there before he tears the place to ribbons."

Jalal eyed her calmly. "You are certain that it is a raccoon?"

"Well, unless a deer got frightened and jumped through the picture window. That's been known to happen. More likely a window got broken somehow and a raccoon got the screen off. Solitaire is empty this week."

He had a vision of a mysterious little animal with a black mask over its eyes. Take a screen off a window? Well, he would like to see that.

"And what if it is not a raccoon?"

"Well?"

"You are setting out to challenge intruders in a remote place, not knowing their numbers, without weapons of any kind?"

Clio blinked.

"And you were surprised to see that I was aboard," he continued ruthlessly. "If I were not here, you would have gone alone on this mission?"

How to explain that she *had* known he was with her, but half unconsciously? How to say that, maybe because she had felt safe with him there, she forgot to stop and consider?

She hardly noticed the curious fact that her unconscious mind was so very far from considering Jalal the enemy.

"Why not?" she said, since that confession was impossible.

He was angry, she could see.

"I'm sure it's a raccoon," she said, half placatingly. "We have to get there fast before he wrecks the place. Raccoons can be worse than thieves half the time." He nodded, unconvinced. "Are you afraid? People around here aren't usually violent, they just rob."

He shook his head. "How many times have you challenged people who are just robbing a cottage?"

She was abashed. She really had acted too quickly, but that was probably Jalal's fault. If he hadn't had her in such a confused state to begin with, she probably wouldn't have been so hasty. He was right—what if it wasn't a raccoon? She looked at the powerful shoulders under the snug-fitting polo shirt and unconsciously relaxed.

"I think Dad surprised some guys once, but they heard the boat and got away before he landed."

He didn't make any comment, instead began looking around him at the boat. "Where is the storage?"

"Some in lockers below, and some under the bench seat at the stern."

He stepped to the stern, and she noticed, not for the first time, how lightly he moved. His body was muscled and well-knit, and when he shifted from one position to another all his muscles seemed to regroup and rebalance. A hunting cat, a panther, she thought, with the promise of power in every economical movement. The tiger had been an appropriate choice of plaque, though she knew he had chosen it only to irritate her.

Meanwhile he moved around, opening lockers. He found a paddle, and his fist closed around it and he hefted it testingly. Satisfied, he returned to the cockpit and slipped into the seat beside her.

No wasted effort. She felt no anxiety from him, just watchfulness. Waiting, like a cat, till the moment when effort would be needed. Then the muscles would bunch and flex, but for now they were long and easy.

She was sure she was completely safe with Jalal, whatever they might find.

"What is the position of Solitaire?" he asked.

She described it to him: an island in a narrow, shallow river, surrounded by forest. At the top end, beyond the island, the river narrowed and became an impassable creek. There was only one way out by water, the way they would go in. A picturesque wooden footbridge led over the water on one side, but only to a footpath that went for miles through the forest before you reached even another cottage.

He took it in in silence, and she could see him building a picture in his mind. She did her best to fill in the details, describing the dock, the approach, the land around the house, even though she was almost sure he was overreacting. There was something about his air of readiness that communicated the more serious possibilities.

"Here's the river mouth," she said at last, and he nodded. His mouth was set, his jaw firm but not clenched.

"You will stay in the boat until I make a check," he said. "You will keep the motor running. If there is danger, you will turn the boat immediately when I tell you, and go to find your father, or the police. Do you understand?"

Clio stiffened. "You aren't in your rebel camp now, Prince Jalal! And I am not one of your followers!"

"No," he agreed calmly. "None of my followers would act so stupidly as this. Nevertheless, you must obey me. If someone captured you, I could do nothing. I would have to surrender if they threatened to hurt you."

Six

It was called Bent Needle River because of its shape. A long ribbon of water looped around an island that formed the eye of the needle. The river twisted at the bottom end of the island, so that from the air its shape was like a darning needle bent sharply just before the eye. Beyond it, a few hundred yards of creek stretched like a short thread trailing from the eye of the needle.

The cottage was on the far side of the island, and the sound of their approach, she knew, would be well muffled by the trees and thick foliage until they were around the bend and almost at the dock. She approached at low speed. The channel was not marked and there were shallows on both sides.

A small motorboat bobbed against the dock, secured only by the stern rope. Goods were stacked on the dock. Clio saw the television set, the video player, a cardboard box. The front door of the wide-windowed cottage gaped open, broken on its hinges. There was more loot collected on the porch.

Not a raccoon, then. She thought of her danger if she had come here alone, and threw Jalal a look as she guided the powerboat quietly around the bend and coasted up to the dock. Just then a man stepped out onto the porch, carrying the vacuum cleaner.

Jalal seemed to take in the whole scene with one comprehensive glance and make up his mind. "Stay in the boat, keep the engine running, and be ready to go if I give you the signal," he commanded quietly. He leapt lightly off the boat onto the dock and stood there, leaning casually on the paddle he had taken with him.

She saw the man break stride for a second, then make up his mind to brazen it out. He kept walking down towards the dock. Thin and wiry, with shoulder-length dirty brown hair, in his forties, she thought. His clothes were grubby but not really dirty—a light grey T-shirt with some kind of logo, black denims.

"Hello there! Can I help you?" he called casually, but too loudly, and she hoped Jalal had picked up the information that there was someone else in the cottage.

"Are you moving out?" she heard Jalal ask, with easy interest.

"Oh, I wish, eh?" The man was grinning self-deprecatingly when she looked again. He clearly did not want to arrive on the dock, but had no choice. He set down the vacuum cleaner and straightened warily.

In the doorway of the house a shadow moved. "Naw, I'm just the hired moving man, eh?"

Jalal nodded. "I understand. But you have the wrong

address. No one is moving from this house. So why don't you get in the boat and go?''

The man feigned indignation. ''Hey, buddy, who ya think you're talking to, eh?'' But Clio could hear his essential weakness in his voice and breathed a sigh of relief. He would bluster and then obey.

Already he was inching towards where his boat was moored.

''I know very well who I am talking to. Now I tell you, you are making a mistake, and you can get in your boat and leave, and your friends, too.''

He raised his voice. ''Why don't you come out? Your friend is leaving and you may go with him.''

A figure appeared in the doorway. ''What the frig's goin' on?'' he said, and Clio's breath hissed in between suddenly clenched teeth. This man was very different from his partner. He was big and muscled, his head shaved, his lower jaw protuberant with low intelligence and aggression. His white singlet and camouflage pants were cleaner than his partner's clothes. He wore a wide belt and hard boots, several metal studs in one ear.

He clumped deliberately down the broad steps from the porch and strode down to the dock with a threatening swagger. Jalal's posture, negligently leaning on the paddle, did not change. The thug stopped a few feet away from him and spat deliberately on the ground.

''Hey, a Ay-rab!'' His eyes swept past Jalal and over Clio with a look that turned her stomach. ''And a skirt!'' But he did not say *skirt*. She shuddered with revulsion. He turned to Jalal again. ''Thanks for bringing my dessert, Saddam! You can go now, less you wanna be the main course.

''Ooooffff!'' The breath seemed to explode out of his body as, almost faster than she could see, Jalal drove the paddle into his solar plexus. The thug seemed to leap into the air and fold in the middle simultaneously.

"Behind you!" Clio screamed, as the smaller man leapt for him, and somehow, instead of connecting, the thin man seemed to sail over Jalal's shoulder as Jalal dropped the paddle, grabbed his arm and assisted his forward motion.

He landed sprawling on the big man, and screamed like an animal, a sound that sent a rush of horror over her skin. His partner threw him impatiently aside, and the reason for the scream was suddenly evident as blood spattered the thug's hands. The thin man had landed skidding on the knife that the thug had pulled from somewhere, and his chest was sliced from shoulder to waist. His T-shirt gaped. Blood poured from the wound.

The wounded man cursed violently. "I'm hurt, man, I'm hurt!"

The thug ignored him and got to his feet. He was sweating. "Okay, Saddam, you shouldna done that. You shouldna made me mad."

Jalal stood with his arms loose at his sides. "Your friend needs a doctor," he said. "Get in your boat and go."

"Jeez, man, I'm hurt bad! Let's do what he says!"

"Drop the boat keys on the dock, Saddam, leave the skirt, get in my boat and take off, and nobody'll get hurt," said the thug to Jalal, as if he hadn't heard his friend's cry.

Jalal said nothing. She could not see his face, but from the back he looked so lightly poised he almost seemed to move with the breeze.

"You hear me, Ay-rab?" The thug began to toss the bloody knife between his two hands, bouncing his weight from foot to foot. He was inches taller than Jalal, and thirty pounds heavier. And clearly he made it his business to be menacing.

Still Jalal made no reply.

"I'm not gonna hurt her, don't you worry none about that. I'm gonna treat her real nice. Whereas you, I'm gonna hurt you bad, if you don't—"

As if he were dancing, Jalal stepped to the side, and his foot arced up, connecting with the thug's right hand as it was in the act of catching the knife. The man cried out with a shriek of pain, and Clio saw with ugly shock that his forearm now bent where it should not. Stumbling forward off balance as he clutched at it with his other hand, he suddenly felt Jalal's hand close on his wrist and his scream changed note. Jalal's other hand fell ruthlessly on his shoulder, and, tripping over the television set, the thug was propelled forward off the dock and down into his boat with a crash.

He screamed in wild, almost demented agony, clutching his shoulder, his arm, his shoulder again, as a stream of curses spewed out of his mouth. His face was cut, his eye already swelling.

"My shoulder!" he screamed, with such a terrible cry that Clio's stomach started to heave again. "My arm!"

Jalal turned back to the other man, who was with difficulty scrambling to his feet, trying to stop the bleeding from his chest with his hands. His eyes widened at whatever he saw in Jalal's face.

"I'm wounded, man! Don't hit me!"

"Get in the boat and take your friend out of here."

Clio gasped at the deadly menace in his voice.

"I can't, man! I can't drive a boat! Man, I'm all cut! You gotta get me to a doctor."

"Get out," Jalal said softly.

The man choked off his protest and stumbled to the

edge of the dock, then let go of his bleeding chest to clamber into the boat. His friend was still screaming in agony. Somehow, the thin man got the motor started on the second try.

"Jeez, the rope! Untie the rope, will ya?" he cried.

Jalal bent to pick up the bloody knife, and with one powerful stroke he chopped down against the wooden dock, severing the rope that tied the boat, as if only now he let his anger escape.

The thin man swore in fear, dragging in the remnant of the rope, and clumsily steered around the powerboat and back down the river. Clio cut her own motor, and they stood listening to the sound retreating in the distance.

Silence fell over them, the silence of wind amongst leaves and of chittering birds. With painfully sweet normality water lapped against the hull of the boat.

"Should we follow them to make sure?" she asked.

Jalal shook his head. "No need."

Her boat was drifting, and almost without conscious thought she started her engines and brought it in to the dock. She threw him the rope and he made it fast, then helped her to come ashore. She accepted his hand, although of course she needed no help. She had been getting in and out of boats all her life.

At the touch of his warm, living flesh, though, she began to tremble.

"Are you all right, Jalal? Were you hurt?" she whispered. "Did he cut you?"

"No. I was not hurt," he said firmly.

"Oh, thank God! Oh, when I saw that knife!"

Jalal took her wordlessly in his arms, and suddenly sensation swept up and engulfed her.

"Jalal!" she breathed hoarsely. "Oh, Jalal!" And she

lifted her face up for the touch of his, wanting to know that he was alive, that he was real.

The tiniest, tenderest smile pulled at his lips, and then he bent and obliged her seeking lips with a gentle kiss. Only then did she remember that barely an hour ago she had sworn she would never want his kiss...but it didn't matter to her. The sweetest relief swept her body at the touch, and she wrapped her arms around him and wished he would kiss her harder....

Then, as if this touch was what she had needed to release the pent-up tension, Clio suddenly began to shake. She was seeing again how the man had looked at her. When Jalal lifted his lips she drew back, squeezing her eyes shut.

"Oh, Jalal, thank God you were here! My God, if I'd come alone!"

"*Alhamdolillah* you didn't come alone. You came with me," he said steadily.

She was shaking all over. He put his arm around her and led her to a bench by the water. "Sit down," he commanded gently, and when she obeyed, he smiled.

"Now I know you are not yourself, when you obey me without protest!"

She smiled, but in spite of herself she felt sick. "I can't stop shaking!" she said.

Jalal sank down beside her and took her in his arms to hold her against his chest. She felt the hot tears prickle her eyes, and let them have their way. She found without surprise that she could cry in front of Jalal. An hour ago she would have said he was the last man on earth she would show weakness to.

He held her while she wept out the tension, the fear, the horror—and maybe something else, which she didn't want to face. "Thank you," she murmured, between sobs. "I'm sorry I have to do this. I can't seem to stop."

He merely held her more tightly.

At last, with a watery smile, she asked, "Do you by any chance have a tissue?" and Jalal let go of her with one arm and searched the pocket of his pants. He found some clean but crushed tissues and handed them to her.

"Are you better now?"

"Much better! Thank you," she said, wiping her eyes. She shuddered. "You could have been killed!"

He smiled grimly. "Not by one like him."

"Oh, God! Wasn't he horrible!"

Jalal's face tightened, but he did not reply.

"I guess we'd better radio the police," she said. "Tell them what to look out for."

"Yes." He nodded. "Radio the police while I look around. Please stay by the boat till I tell you it is clear."

He straightened and moved quickly up towards the cottage.

Clio climbed back aboard the boat, punched up the police channel and made a report, then radioed home. The radio wasn't always on at home, but it would be on now, with the kids nearby, waiting for news. When Ben answered, Clio told him what had happened and then kept him on the line till Jalal reappeared and signalled her that everything was clear.

"Okay, Ben, I'll call you again when we're on our way back," she said, and put the radio on standby.

"How bad is it?" she asked, meeting Jalal on the dock.

"Not bad," he said. "They did not deliberately vandalize the place." She sighed her relief.

They began to restore order, carrying the looted items back inside the cottage, plugging things in. An observer might have noticed how coordinated their work was, how easily each seemed to understand the other's intentions and assist, but Clio didn't consciously notice. When Jalal began to lift chunks of broken mirror from the bedroom wardrobe door, it was natural to her to bring in the big garbage can so he could drop the pieces straight in. And when the job was finished and she swept up the remnants of glass, she found him bending with the dustpan when she needed it, without surprise.

That night they had to recount their adventures over the dinner table, to a fascinated audience. Brandon had eaten quickly and returned to Solitaire with Jonah for repairs. All the remaining children sat around the table.

The police had come and dusted for fingerprints, and had gone away with the bloody knife. Tonight Brandon would board it up, tomorrow a new front door would be installed, and the mirror, ready for the renters on the weekend.

So it was only a thrilling story, and the kids were enthralled by it. It went without saying the part they were most enthralled by was Jalal's "kung fu magic," as they insisted on calling it.

"Did you study self-defence, Jalal?" Ben asked. He was more than halfway down the road to hero worship, Clio could see. She wanted to resent it, but how could she? After this afternoon, how could she say anything to dim their admiration? If Jalal had not been here, would she have gone to Solitaire alone when the alarm went? Or maybe with only Ben for company?

She was a mess of conflicting feelings and ideas. He had kidnapped Zara and held her hostage, but he had also saved Clio from an experience so awful she could not bear to think of it. These two images of Jalal couldn't be reconciled. She could only leap back and forth between them, in a dizzying contradiction that made her brain hurt.

When she tuned in to the conversation again, Jalal was agreeing to teach Ben the rudiments of the art of self-defence, and all the others were chiming in with pleas not to be excluded.

"I can teach one or teach all," Jalal said pacifyingly. "We can do it, but—!" His forefinger went up, and they all gazed at him intently, as if every word out of his mouth held magic. "Everyone comes to every class, unless for a very good reason. If you want to do this, then we do it. But it involves discipline."

They all nodded solemnly at this expression of authority, and abruptly Clio was angry. Was the man going to start recruiting followers right in the family?

"Did you teach your supporters self-defence?" she asked, after the kids rushed off in a body to clear out a room and find some mattresses.

He heard the hostility under her tone and frowned thoughtfully as he looked across the table at her. They were alone in the big kitchen. Sunset was slanting through the windows. She could hear crickets screeching, and a boat went past far out on the lake. They sat in shadows, watching each other.

"Yes, many of them learned."

"What a pity Zara never took a course in self-defence."

"Your sister is a brave and resourceful woman, but self-defence would have been of little use to her in such a situation."

"You admired her, then. How deep did the admiration go?"

"Too deep to do to her what that thug would have done to you today. Do you equate me with him in your mind?"

Clio closed her eyes. Did she? Why was she baiting him, after what he had done today?

"Is what you did so different?" she asked. Her feelings were deeply confused. She didn't understand herself at all.

His jaw tight, Jalal got to his feet. "If you do not trust me, Clio, it is because you do not trust yourself. In your heart you know the truth. It is not me, but your own heart that you do not trust. Ask yourself why."

She heard his quiet tread up the stairs, heard the children call out to him, heard a door close.

Clio sat alone in the deepening shadows for a long while, and then one of the dogs, sensing her distress and confusion, pushed a cold, wet, sympathetic nose into her hand.

Everyone had forgotten their table-clearing duties in the excitement, but for once she would let it go. She was grateful for the activity, as well as the solitude. She stacked the dishwasher without putting the lights on, cleared the table, tidied the kitchen. She spent a few minutes liberally dousing herself with insect repellent and pulled on a light jacket. Then she picked up the dogs' leashes and pushed open the screen door onto the evening.

They tumbled out ahead of her, and set off along her usual path, following the line of the shore away from the town, climbing. After a while, she came out onto her favourite vantage point, a clearing on a hillside overlooking the lake, where the dogs immediately began to chase and play. She sat on her favourite rock, watching as the lights came on in the town of Love's Point and in cottages all around the lake.

Ask yourself why.

Seven

Madeleine Donnelly and Brandon Blake had come separately to Love's Point in the sixties, when it had been a centre for hippie culture. They had met and fallen in love during their first summer there, when Maddy was painting chalk portraits for tourists, and Brandon played the guitar.

A few years later, in a wild venture, they decided to buy the ramshackle, almost derelict old Love house with a mortgage their parents gave them, and restore it. The Love house had been built by the family who had come here in the nineteenth century and given their name to the point. Once a summer playground for Toronto's old money, Love's Point had fallen on hard times with the Depression, and the big Victorian house had been for a while a cheap hotel. By the late sixties it had been virtually abandoned.

Now, thirty years on, the place was a landmark again, and the Blakes, like the Loves before them, ''owned half the lake.'' A marina, an ice cream parlour, rental cottages around the area, a pioneer cabin museum with a barn turned into an artisans' studio and craft shop where you could go to watch craftspeople working in the old ways, and Maddy's special baby, an increasingly important art gallery showing mostly First Nation art, were all part of the casual, sprawling Blake empire.

When the house was about half finished, Maddy and Brandon had decided the time had come for children, and once they started there just didn't seem to be any reason to stop. There was always another bedroom to fill. Now there were nine Blakes, of whom the two eldest had departed for the city—but that was never the end of the story. For the Blake brood had an endless supply of cousins and friends, and somehow or other there was always a reason why someone was moving in for a while.

At twenty-two, Clio was third oldest. Zara and Jude had both left home for the bright lights, and Clio knew people were thinking her turn was next. But Clio wasn't going anywhere. Love Lake and the area around it was her spiritual home. She was one of the lucky ones. She had been born right where she belonged.

While her sister Zara had dreamed of foreign travel, of seeing all the strange places they read about in books, Clio had dreamed of being married, of having lots of babies, like her mother. Her dreams of career reached no further than someday managing her mother's art gallery as she now managed the ice cream store. She always loved meeting the dark-eyed artists who spoke familiarly of their spirit guides and spirit places, and whose paintings were not ordinary landscapes, or distant places, but different ways of seeing what was right under your nose.

For Clio, now, as for the artists, nature was alive with

the spirits of Bear, Wolf, Coyote, Beaver, and a dozen others.

The bright lights held little attraction for her. She could understand the yearnings that Zara and Jude felt, but she did not share them. Everything she wanted had always been within her reach.

Everything but one thing.

She had first seen Peter Clifford on her first day of high school, and she had fallen in love with him the same moment. Peter was in his final year. He was handsome, with thick dark blond hair and wicked hazel eyes, and a body to die for.

It didn't take her long to find out that every day after school he went down to his father's car dealership…. It didn't take her long, either, to work out that the bus route from the high school to Love's Point went right by Clif*Ford*'s. After that, several times a week after school, Clio walked three bus stops down the road, past the car dealership, before catching her bus. She was almost always rewarded with the sight of Peter in the forecourt or through the window.

He often seemed to notice her, almost as if he was looking out for her. When he waved to her, Clio's day was made.

When Peter and Zara started dating, Clio almost didn't mind. No one in the family knew how she felt about Peter, so it wasn't as though Zara was poaching. And it seemed only fair that her fabulous sister should get the handsomest boy around. Anyway, Clio had always known that she was too young and ordinary to really interest Peter.

Zara's relationship with him was very casual. The last thing Zara wanted, she told Clio, was to get involved with a local boy without any ambition of his own, who would want to tie her down.

Clio was fifteen when her adored older sister went off to university. And then the magic she had dreamed of happened. Within two weeks of Zara's departure, Clio, walking as usual past the car dealership, stopped in on an impulse to say hi...and Peter suddenly seemed to *see* her for the first time.

"Hey, Clio, you're all grown up all of a sudden," he said, with a smile on his face that melted her where she stood.

"You just noticed?" she returned flippantly, over a heartbeat that was drowning out the world.

"You're almost as beautiful as your sister," he said, and, fool that she was, she had taken it as a compliment.

He asked her out on a date, and that night, in his fabulous sporty convertible, tickling her cheek and ear with one lazy hand while he expertly drove with the other, he told her again how gorgeous she was, now that she was all grown up.

They dated all that fall, more and more often, and with more and more intensity in the passionate kisses they exchanged. She thrilled to his touch, as crazy to be near him as he was to be near her.

When she looked back on that time now, those wild, wild responses, it felt like a dream. Had she really felt like that, or had she imagined it, because that was the way she thought it should be?

He always stopped short of actual lovemaking. "Not yet, sweetheart," he would whisper, because Clio was so young, so innocent, so crazy for him she couldn't have denied him anything he wanted.

She knew Peter really cared for her, because he was so determined to wait. She knew from her friends that not every guy was so unselfish, not by a long chalk.

She imagined—she was almost certain—that he was

waiting till they could become engaged. They were too young now, of course, nineteen and fifteen! But twenty and sixteen…oh, Clio thought, what a world of difference there would be when Peter was twenty and she was sixteen!

When her mother started worrying that Clio was getting in deep with a guy too old for her, she assured Maddy that Peter had serious intentions, and was waiting. He wasn't trying to pressure her into early sex at all….

He turned twenty in November. Clio's own birthday was in December.

On her sixteenth birthday Peter took Clio out to a special restaurant, in a neighbouring town, wining and dining her like the grown-up woman she now was, and she smiled into his melting look and knew that Peter had made up his mind that it would be tonight. Tonight… She wondered if he had already bought the ring….

They went straight to a motel from the restaurant. Her body had been melting for miles. And when he closed the door and locked it behind them, and took her into his arms, she heard his passionate indrawn breath and chills of excitement poured over her….

It was when he was at last lying beside her, his eyes closed, kissing her, fondling her breasts, when heart and body were melting and singing with love and desire, that she heard it.

"Zara," he whispered. Like a drunk man, although he wasn't drunk. Slurring the word. "Zara."

"Peter!" She had tugged at his chin, making him look at her. "Peter, what did you say?" She smiled frowningly at him.

"Oh, baby! Oh, baby! I'm sorry, but you always knew, didn't you?"

She would never forget how her heart started beating

in that moment. She knew that she would never be able to wipe it from her memory, not if she lived to be a hundred, like the old medicine woman on the reserve....

"Knew?"

"I've been dying for you, sweetheart, she never let me!"

She did not resist what happened next. Now, when she thought of the strange passivity that had invaded her at his words, she supposed she had been in a kind of shock.

Whatever caused it, she hadn't fought him, and it wasn't rape. She had felt invaded, used...but it wasn't rape, she knew that, even if it was the worst thing she'd ever experienced in her life....

Afterwards, lying there, she had wept. *I thought it was what you wanted,* he had said sulkily. And she responded, helpless in the face of such blank ignorance, *Not like this.*

There was worse to come. When he drove her home, just as if she could possibly be interested, he told her how deeply he loved Zara. "As crazy for her as you've always been for me," he said.

With a new cynicism, she asked, "Why did you wait? If all you wanted was a second-class Zara, why wait so long?" He had to know she would have given him whatever he asked for weeks ago.

He smiled at her naivete.

"Baby, you were jailbait, remember? I knew you were crazy for it, but hey! Fifteen years old! Tonight you became a consenting adult."

Clio sat up. The moon was climbing up the darkening sky, and the dogs were snuffling at something interesting in the bushes. They never seemed to learn that such an interest almost always resulted in a scratched nose...or worse.

"Come on, Buddy, Frowner!" she called, not at all wanting to have to deal with skunked dog tonight.

Was there something wrong with her, that she was attracted to such men as Peter and Jalal? Men who could use a woman entirely for their own purposes, without stopping to consider her feelings?

Still, Jalal was wrong when he accused her of blaming him because she couldn't face what Peter had done to her. Peter had hurt her, all right, but he hadn't raped her, and she had never hidden from the memory. She'd never told anyone, but she hadn't pretended it hadn't happened or anything like that.

She was wary of Jalal because of what he himself had done. She wasn't loading him with Peter's—or anyone else's—sins. He had his own, whether he wanted to face it or not

Anyway, she wasn't attracted to Jalal. It was hardly a statement of undying love if in her relief this afternoon she had wanted to kiss him! That was just an automatic human response, wanting to reaffirm life when death had seemed so close. Everybody knew sex and death were like two sides of the same coin.

Her mind slipped to the thug at Solitaire, and with a shiver of sick dread she remembered the way his eyes had travelled over her. She might still be his prisoner, subjected to whatever horror he could think of...if Jalal hadn't been with her.

She had seen in Jalal's eyes how much he despised the man. The involuntary escape of rage that she had seen, when the knife came down and severed the rope, had made her gasp, had terrified the little man in the boat.

Was it a form of self-hatred? Had he seen himself in another form?

Clio shook her head, but that didn't clear it. The moon

was high, the mosquitoes ravenous, and at home they would be wondering where she was. She stood and whistled to the dogs, and set off on the path home.

"Assalaamu aleikum." The voice crackled in his ear.

Jalal hesitated, glancing around the darkened hallway. *"Waleikum assalaam."*

"You know my voice, I think."

He relaxed at this use of the code. "There is news?"

"A rumour has surfaced."

He was silent, waiting. The window at the end of the hall stood wide open onto the night, but his voice would not carry so far.

"A rumour that says you have been secretly sent into exile by the princes, your uncles, and that your silence on the subject is the price of your life."

Jalal stood silent in the shadows as the soft wind caressed the trees.

"It may mean danger."

He smiled. "What is the reason given for my banishment?"

Soft laughter. "What else? That you were intriguing for the throne of Barakat."

"Ah."

"Be on your guard. *Ma'assalaam.*"

"Ma'assalaam," Jalal repeated, and quietly replaced the receiver.

As she came out of the trees the dogs rushed to the verandah in the darkness, waggling their backsides as if they wanted to break their spines in two, making happy whines in their throats. Clio stiffened. Her skin shivered to attention. She knew it was him.

"Dad?" she queried anyway, as she came up the steps.

Jalal's voice came out of the darkness. "He has taken everyone out for a ride on the lake."

"You didn't go?" Another shiver coursed through her.

"As you see."

He sounded harsh. Usually his voice stroked her. The verandah was deep in gloom, out of reach of the moonlight. With one foot on the top step, she paused, almost afraid to enter the darkness where he waited.

If he tried to make love to her now, what would she do?

She was outlined in moonlight as she hesitated there, nervous, as if at the entrance to the cave of some wild animal. Jalal's blood leapt angrily. Why did she persist in thinking of him as she did? He was not a man of violence. Had he not proven his worth to her today? In just such a way would he have dealt with any of his own followers who had tried to harm her sister. The episode should have shown her what a gulf existed between himself and the sort of filthy infidel he had protected her from.

She had asked for his kiss afterwards, as reassurance. Could she be unaware of the meaning of her own actions?

Her legs were long and their shape was revealed by the fine cloth of the striped *shalwar* she wore, pants that ended below the knee. The old Mughal paintings showed women of the harem in such pants, inviting a man to start at the delicate, jewelled feet, the naked ankles and calves, and work his way up....

Jalal's jaw clenched. She stood there quivering, thinking her response due to fear, but he knew it was at the promise of delight.

"What do you fear?" he asked roughly.

She started, listening alertly, like a wild deer that instinctively feels the sights of the hunter's gun.

"Wh-what?" she whispered.

"I kissed you today," he continued, his voice harsh. "Do you fear me because of it?"

"Yes…no," she murmured helplessly, still frozen there in moonlight.

Her stomach was bare, exactly as in those antique erotic paintings. Only the jewel in the navel was missing. He could imagine the texture of the underside of her breasts behind the little top, so near to a seeking hand….

"Do you fear that we will feel more pleasure than you can bear, Clio?"

Her breath hissed audibly. As her eyes became accustomed to the gloom of the verandah, she could see the faint outline of him. He sat on the battered old rattan settee, his arms spread along the back, his knees wide apart. Even in the darkness she felt the impact of this offering of his sex to her. His presence was unmistakably male, as if some masculine perfume enveloped her, which she could not quite smell….

"No," she said. She could almost have laughed at the idea. But somehow she couldn't laugh, couldn't tell him how far from correct his assessment of her sexual capacity was.

"The promise of overwhelming pleasure between a man and a woman is rare," he whispered, as if she hadn't answered. "I, too, almost fear it. This is natural, perhaps, but the old poets swear that to lose the self in the moment of union is a gift. Shall we prove together that it is so?"

She watched the shadow of his arm detach itself from the gloom and reach out to her. She licked her lips, unable to speak.

"Clio," he commanded softly, almost irresistibly. "Let me show you the root of your fear of me."

A door opened in the distance and a few faint bars of music reached them before being abruptly cut off again.

In the dying lilacs a sleepy bird briefly queried whether it was morning.

Caught in the beam of his masculinity, she could hardly breathe.

"I know what it is I fear," she said. But her voice was hoarse when she had meant it to be strong. Her body was coursing with icy sensation, yet she knew the air around her was still warm.

"And convince you that it is not to be feared," Jalal murmured. A greedy beam of moonlight caught and caressed a dark curl as he moved his head. She felt a sudden pain, as if one could be jealous of a moonbeam.

She shook her head, to clear it of such insanity.

"It's not pleasure I fear!"

The rattan creaked. She stiffened in alarm, but he had merely withdrawn his arm and replaced it on the back of the settee.

"What, then?"

"How arrogant you are!" she marvelled, as fury released her from the need to recognize something that had almost surfaced.

He could feel his own impatient anger vying with the desire that burned in his heart and loins.

"First kiss me, and then tell me that I am wrong," he growled.

As if this were a direct physical threat, she leapt up the last step and quickly crossed the verandah to the screen door. In the kitchen a night-light gave quiet promise of refuge.

She half expected that he would get up and challenge her, but when she dragged open the screen and slipped through, Prince Jalal did not move from his seat.

Eight

The next day, Maddy Blake returned from her buying trip with a vanload of paintings, carvings, dream catchers, jewellery, beadwork and deerskin items of all kinds. Everyone helped unload and unpack, oohing and aahing as the season's catch was revealed.

"I'm starting a new line—deerskin clothes," Maddy announced, displaying several items that had the girls gasping with delight.

"I'm trying that on!" "Oh, and that!" "Me, too!" Clio and Rosalie and Arwen exclaimed at a rate of about once every two minutes.

"I'm twying that on!" Donnelly exclaimed in her turn, as an adorable little fringed skirt and vest in soft white deerskin with delicate turquoise and red beading came out of the wrappings.

Maddy smiled. "I'm glad you like it, darling, because I bought it just for you!" Everyone laughed at the face of exaggerated surprise and pleasure Donnelly made, her eyes big, her mouth a perfect O.

"Look at this! Oh, this is so sexy!" cried Rosalie next, pulling out a man's black cowhide cowboy hat with a beautiful beadwork band and a small feather. "Here, Jalal, you try it on!"

And suiting the action to the word, she put it on his head and stepped back to admire him.

"Oh, you're so handsome!" she exclaimed, in a voice that showed she was at least halfway to losing her heart.

Clio clenched her jaw, glancing back and forth between the two. She suddenly saw a danger she hadn't foreseen. She wondered how Jalal was taking that. It was hard enough to guess how even the guy next door would take such adoration from a girl almost of consenting age. Jalal was a total stranger to the culture. His rules would be an impenetrable mystery.

"Oh, all the tourist women are just gonna love you!" Rosalie continued. "You could sell them anything!"

It was a disguised way of saying *I love you,* and Clio's heart thudded. Poor Rosalie! It was impossible to disguise love at that age. She must have been just that obvious with her crush on Peter. Afterwards it had been a source of the deepest humiliation to know that he had always seen right through her.

She had spent a long time awake last night, thinking.

Jalal was wrong when he thought—if he really did think it!—that she wanted him. Or that what frightened her was the potential passion between them. She did not have any passion, potential or actual, in her.

Sometimes she wondered, looking back such a long way, if she had ever really *physically* wanted Peter. Perhaps it had been a kind of dream of wanting?

Certainly after that night she had never felt serious sex-

ual desire for a man again. Nothing again had touched her
so deeply. The most she felt had been a kind of detached
physical urge and, understanding that that was all she
would ever feel, she had learned to believe that it would
do.

She had no doubt that other women felt more than she
did. Maybe much more. For sure not a single love song
or poem could ever have been written and sustained on
any passion Clio felt, so there must be more.

Men were annoyed by her coolness under fire, yet she
was grateful and polite about the pleasure they gave her—
why wasn't it enough?

A boyfriend had said once, "There is another woman
in there, Clio, I know there is!" but if so he had never
reached her.

Even Peter hadn't been able to reignite the feelings she
had once thought she had for him. He had wanted to try,
but she couldn't understand why. "But, Peter, what's the
point?" she had asked coolly, when he had tried to kiss
her. "I'm not Zara. I never will be."

"Clio, you love me!" he had exploded. "And I'm finally coming to realize maybe it was you I loved all
along!"

She had smiled, almost laughed, at that.

So she had no fears about Jalal stirring up depths in her
she couldn't control. She was a woman without much sex
drive, and it was going to take more than a handsome
Arab sheikh to change that.

Now Jalal smiled lazily as they all admired him, telling
him he looked like one of the *coureurs de bois,* those
intrepid explorers of Canada's past.

He really is a wonderful-looking guy, she thought. The
sight of him hurt her somehow. *Handsome and strong and*

much more macho than Peter ever was… Gorgeous! No wonder Rosalie's falling for him!

Jalal said something and took off the hat, setting it on Rosalie's head. Like one of the family already, except that the look Rosalie gave him wasn't one anyone gave a brother…Clio couldn't be sure what was in Jalal's eyes when he smiled back.

Her heart began to beat with the deep trouble she felt— hard, slow thuds that frightened her. How would Jalal react if Rosalie made it so clear she adored him? He said he wanted Clio…would he take Rosalie as a substitute? Was she watching history about to repeat itself?

On Saturday the ice cream shop, the crafts shop and the art gallery went on full-time summer hours, and within a couple of weeks the season was in full swing.

Generally speaking, the boys helped out Brandon at the marina and the tackle shop, and the girls looked after the ice cream shop, the craft store and the art gallery. They shared duty at the barn. For years, this had made Maddy despair. Her feminist impulses hated to see such clear sex-linked leanings.

"Couldn't *one* of you try for a little cross-gender interest?" she sometimes wailed.

Not that Clio didn't like working on boats and motors, or minded selling bait—on those occasions when her father needed an extra hand, or when business in the boutiques was slow, she enjoyed messing in the marina.

But this year she had certainly been avoiding it.

Blake's Marina sold, repaired and rented boats and tackle. Sometimes inexperienced tourists wanted someone to take them out fishing, and Brandon accommodated them when he could.

For the last few years, Jude had split this job with his

father, and Ben was now in line for it. But Ben was not allowed to take anyone out alone till he was eighteen, and Brandon had given Jalal a crash course so he could fill the vacancy.

Ben always wanted to go along on such fishing trips, and whenever there was a chance, Clio was certain to get a request from a panting Ben for someone to take his place in the marina for a couple of hours....

"Who's taking them?" Clio asked, one wet morning in early July, as she stood behind the ice cream counter facing another such request.

"Dad, I think," Ben said. "Come on, Clio, they only want a short trip, and you won't get much business here till the sun comes out. Anyway, Jalal knows what he's doing, he'll hardly need you."

Clio hesitated as Rosalie came running in from the craft shop.

"Clio, I don't mind doing it!" she said, with a praise-worthy attempt at casualness.

Clio did not want to go and spend two hours with Jalal in a not very busy marina on a day when it was probably going to rain. For a moment she weighed the probable damage to Rosalie of that time alone with Jalal against her own disinclination.

Then she reached behind her and, to Rosalie's evident disappointment, began to untie the white baker's apron that covered her T-shirt and pedal pushers.

"Thanks, Rosalie, but Jalal's really not very experienced yet, and neither are you. You can cover here and leave the craft shop to Isabel. It won't get busy. If you have any problems, send Arwen over to the gallery for Mom, okay?"

Rosalie's chin sank, and she nodded wordlessly. Clio

felt like a heel, but as the old phrase had it, *This is hurting me more than you.* She was doing her cousin a favour.

Her heart anxious, Clio followed Ben along the boardwalk that led from the house to the marina.

Two men were standing on the dock above one of the fishing boats, but it was Jalal, not her father, who was aboard, loading the fishing tackle.

Clio blinked and looked again, then stopped a few yards away, catching her breath on an astonished grin.

It was like a scene from a movie. Two dark-haired, swarthy-skinned men in navy *business suits* stood on the dock among the boxes of tackle, looking as out of place as if they had just flown in from Mars.

"Ben, who *are* they?" she asked in a whisper.

But Ben did not stop. He surged ahead, crying, "Oh, great! Jalal's going to take them! Jalal!" he called. "Are you going out with them?"

Jalal, expertly stowing a tackle box aboard, looked up and nodded. "Yes, I'm taking them out." He already seemed totally at home in this environment, Clio realized. Maybe boats were in his genes.

"Great! I can go with you. Clio's going to cover for me," said the boy, jumping aboard and immediately starting to help stow the gear.

"Laa! Laa!" bleated a guttural voice above him, as one of the men turned to the other in a babble of protest.

"The boy does not come," the other man translated to Jalal, in English. "No one comes. No room."

Jalal glanced impassively from one to the other. "All right," he said. Clio thought admiringly, *No one could guess what you are thinking.*

The customer was always right, but it was certainly the first time any customer had ever rejected the help of a spare, unpaid-for hand. Nodding sadly, Ben helped stow

the last couple of items and then climbed out of the boat
again.

The two men stepped awkwardly into the boat, as if
they had never performed the action before, and under
Jalal's instruction put on life vests over their suit jackets.
They now looked even more ludicrous.

Heck, they're even wearing dress shoes! Clio noted in
amusement. She stood watching while Ben tossed Jalal
the ropes and then pushed them off with his foot.

Jalal put the engine in gear and eased away from the
dock.

The eyes of the two men suddenly raked Clio in rude
assessment, and one said something to the other that made
her flesh creep even though she couldn't understand the
actual words.

She saw Jalal's jaw tighten, and the boat turned, too
sharply and too fast, causing the men to stagger and clutch
each other for balance, ruffling their male dignity. Seconds later, the boat was heading out into the lake. Clio
stood staring after it, her brain whirling with speculation.

The men and Jalal had all acted as if the only language
they had in common was English. But Clio was almost
sure that the language the two men were speaking between themselves was Arabic.

She was absolutely certain that, whatever language it
was, Jalal understood every word they spoke. And that,
for all their careful pretence otherwise, the men knew it.

Who were they? What business could they have with
Jalal?

Nine

"**J**alal, I *can't!*"

Clio froze, her ears pricked, not sure what she had heard. Her heart kicked uncomfortably.

She had had a long, hard day. One of the high school girls had not shown for her evening shift in the ice cream shop, and after a full working day, Clio had had to fill in for her. Her parents were out at a meeting. Clio had missed the evening meal, and when she came in she had gone straight upstairs to the attic room where she slept, to relax in a warm bath. Now, in her bathrobe, she was on her way down the back stairs to find something in the fridge to tide her over till morning

Rosalie's voice had come from behind a closed door. Barefoot, Clio crept along the passage, listening intently to locate the room.

"But won't it hurt?"

A man laughed softly. "Only a little," said Jalal, his

voice seductively reassuring. Clio only just caught the words, and her heart clenched spasmodically. She couldn't believe her ears.

This was far worse than anything she had imagined. She had imagined him breaking Rosalie's heart, but not—!

Maybe she should have known. Maybe a man who would take a hostage wasn't above anything.

"But—"

She stopped outside the door. It wasn't Rosalie's room. She wasn't sure whose it might be. The two or three empty rooms on this floor and the next one down were filled by whatever cousin or friend had come to stay temporarily, on a regularly changing rota.

"Think—you will get hurt if you don't. Come, now, Rosalie. Be brave."

Her stomach twisting, her heart beating in her ears like thunder, Clio wrapped her hand around the doorknob and silently turned it. Her heart's thunder was so loud she could barely hear anything else, and her chest was so powerfully constricted she could take only the shallowest breath.

"I *can't!*"

The door moved by quarter inches, while she prayed for strength. When she saw them at last, directly in her line of vision, her heart contracted with almost desperate pain.

They stood on the far side of a mattress that was on the floor between them and the door. Jalal had Rosalie in a firm grip, one arm around her neck, the other hand clasping her arm above the elbow. She had her head tilted up over her shoulder towards him, and he was smiling down at her with seductive encouragement.

They were both too absorbed to notice her.

"Think of Arwen, then!" Jalal urged. "Think what might happen to her if you don't!"

Arwen? This was worse than she could have imagined in a week of black fantasies. Rage electrified her, consumed her, obliterating everything except hatred. Clio launched herself, just as, goaded at last into action, Rosalie moved an arm sharply and dropped to one knee, sending Jalal flying in a graceful arc over her head.

Clio, darting full tilt towards them, screeched with astonished admiration, and on the other side of the mattress Rosalie saw her and stared, mouth open.

"Excellent!" Jalal cried.

He landed on the mattress spread-eagled neatly on his back, in time to receive Clio, who, trying to stop her forward progress, made a misstep, tripped on the mattress's near edge and fell.

Her knees landed between his spread legs, her outstretched hands slammed against his shoulders, then slid down into the mattress. Momentum drove her body down against his. Her face ended up buried beside his neck, where she was conscious of his breath tickling her ear. Her hair lay tousled over his face, the rich turquoise-and-purple fabric of her bathrobe splayed out around them.

Jalal, with the honed, split-second reactions of a trained fighter, instantly wrapped his arms around her.

There was a moment of stunned silence from everyone. Then, covered in foolish confusion, Clio steeled herself for ridicule and lifted her head. She heaved for breath.

Above her Rosalie was still staring at her like a fish. Beneath her, Jalal was smiling broadly, his teeth white against his tanned skin.

"Class dismissed," he said, and her ears were filled with ringing laughter like the peal of church bells.

"What—" she began stupidly. "What on earth—?"

They lay staring into each other's eyes, while his body shook with laughter, and she felt as if something as real and physical as electricity shot into her from him.

His body stirred urgently against hers. Fire seemed to whoosh through her. Jalal's lips lost their smile and parted and his eyes darkened with hunger.

Clio gasped, assailed from too many directions at once, and stupidly turned her head in the direction of the chiming laughter.

Every member of the household save her parents was sitting against one wall of the room. Their sparkling eyes were fixed on her, their mouths open wide, teeth glinting with delight.

"What on earth is going on?" Clio finally managed to mutter weakly, just as her brain finished its interpretation of events and offered the answer.

This was one of his self-defence classes. How stupid could she get?

She was wearing only a short, silky nightdress under the open robe, and he was wearing the white trousers of his judo *gi*. Nothing, not even a zipper, got in the way of the hard, intimate pressure. Nothing disguised the hot, unfamiliar reaction of her own body, either. The touch of his hand was light now, against the curve of her back, and she wanted it to move lower, to press her against him.

"Let me up," she muttered.

She was drowned out by a chorus of voices all demanding to know what she had been trying to do. She shook her head, because of course she could not tell them the truth. She felt like every kind of idiot under the sun, but what story could she possibly invent that would be in the least plausible to cover such bizarre and astonishing behaviour?

"Let me up," she repeated.

He raised a quizzical eyebrow, and of course he wasn't doing anything to prevent her getting up. If she felt trapped there, it was by her own wishes. Clio jerked away from him, kneeling and then getting to her feet, twitched her bathrobe around her, tossed her loose hair back. After the first impossible-to-resist urge to look, her eyes resolutely stayed away from his groin.

With a reluctant, lazy smile of his heavy-lidded eyes that burned her where she stood, Jalal also flung himself to his feet.

"What kind of an attack was that?" the kids were still demanding, and she realized dimly that all those messages between their bodies had been the work of an instant. It had felt like long minutes.

"Never mind," Clio said with dignity. "It didn't work, my timing was off." She thought how impossibly unfair it would be to let the kids get any idea of her momentary suspicion of Jalal. How confused and unhappy it would make them all, to know that Clio had actually believed Jalal was trying to force Rosalie!

She could not do that to them, shake their trust in a friend—in their hero! she told herself. And then, with the clarity that sometimes comes in the wake of such powerful emotion, she saw the truth.

The truth was that Jalal was not her enemy. He was right: she had made it up because of fear. She was afraid of him because she was sexually attracted to him. That was the whole truth.

A weight seemed to drop away from her. And as it did so, just as arms that have unnaturally strained against an immovable weight will rise unbidden when the weight is released, her spirit seemed to lift.

As that happened, she was invaded by a sweet, melting wave of pure sensuality that filled her entire being, so that she seemed to be floating on the sea of her own limitless being.

She gasped with astonished joy. Never had body and spirit been a source of such pure delight.

Meanwhile the kids were all on their feet, chatting and laughing about how Clio's wild, crazy entrance onto the scene had stunned them.

"Next time!" Jalal called, signalling the breakup of the class for this evening, and to Clio's only faint surprise, the children instantly fell into two neat lines totally unlike their usual rowdy indiscipline and in perfect unison made a smart obeisance before calling their good-nights and filing out of the room. Even Donnelly.

"Come on, Donnelly, bedtime," Rosalie called.

"Okay. Good night, Pwince Jalal."

"Good night, Donnelly," he said.

"So they bow to Prince Jalal after all?" she observed, as Ben, the last one out, closed the door.

"To make respectful obeisance to the teacher is part of the discipline of a fighter," he said. "Just so must one submit one's will to doing only right before one uses the powers and abilities that are taught."

"And did you submit to the necessity of doing only right?" she asked, groping for a familiar support in a new world.

"No," Jalal said softly. "No, Clio, do not hide in this way."

The sun was setting; the room was soft with shadows now.

She turned as if to leave, but his hands caught her, drew her into his arms. "Why do you do it?" he murmured. "Why do you tempt me and then call me a monster? Why is your fear so great?"

Oh, this was too soon. She hadn't had time to collect her thoughts yet. She needed to go away and think.

His hands expertly found the opening of her robe, slipped inside. She started shivering uncontrollably. Distractedly Clio hoped the weather wasn't going to turn cold just in time for the weekend.

"What do you want?" he whispered seductively.

"I don't want anything," she said, and even she could hear the lie. The unbearable lightness of her being began to shimmer and coalesce into a new shape.

"No?" He paused, gazing at her eyes, her face, her lips. "You are not polite, you do not ask me what I want, Clio."

She could remain silent, but she would have needed the help of horses to get her out of that room, out of his arms. She mentally ordered herself to go, but it was futile.

"What then? In this culture I must ask for permission to kiss you? I do not like this. A woman knows what she wants, why is it not also for the woman to ask permission of the man? Or to make demands? Why is only the man understood to have desires? In my country we know better than this."

She licked her dry lips, hardly aware of what he said. It was only the vehicle for the sound. His voice was seductively rough, like a kitten's tongue. Her skin leapt with little shivers of delight and anticipation. She knew she should not answer him; he would only confuse her further if she did.

"Women can ask for what they want," she said anyway.

"Ask me to kiss you, then," he commanded, in a voice so indescribably delicious to the senses she instinctively stopped breathing, to better concentrate on the sensations it aroused in her.

Oh, such sensations as she could hardly remember having felt before. As if she had been born only a minute ago, it was all so new—yet she also knew she had been starved of such feelings for a long, barren lifetime.

All this time his arms were around her, intimately warm through the delicate silk slip that served her as nightwear, holding her only lightly, but with the promise of power in every muscle. One hand on her back, the other inescapably across her hips. She felt the agile strength of his fingers, understood with the direct physical knowledge of her body's hunger how easily he could slip the pale turquoise silk up a few inches to expose her naked thighs to his expert touch....

Oh, but shouldn't she take time? This was all so new, shouldn't she go away and think over what it meant? If it turned out she was a highly sexed woman after all, didn't she have to consider what to do about that?

"No," she muttered weakly, in answer to his command.

He showed her his teeth then, drawing her lower body gently against his, pressing oh so lightly against that heat, so that she could learn, if she had doubted it, that he was still hard, and she was still melting, with desire.

Her sudden indrawn breath rasped in her open throat and her eyes widened, unconsciously inviting him into her being. The hungry blackness of his eyes thrust and probed her deepest self, until she understood the necessity of his body also entering hers.

"I think the men of this culture are not such fools as you tell me," Jalal murmured, and then, inevitably, his head moved closer and his mouth covered hers.

Wild, delicious sensation poured over her. His hands

moved against her back under the robe, just enough to make the silk of her own thin shift caress her skin. The silk belonged to her, perhaps, but the heat was all his.

It coursed over and through her system, a sensual brushstroke that clouded her thoughts, made her glow with delight.

His mouth was a whole gallery of artistic expertise, exploding on the tiny canvas of her lips. He stroked, he brushed, he licked, he dabbled, and meanwhile she saw all the colours of the most inventive palette imaginable. Rich blues, haunting turquoises, deep greens, sensual pinks, erotic purples drowned her, and gold and silver burst and shot across her vision while she sank to a place in herself she did not know.

Her spirit soared free. Laughter and delight bubbled in her.

Her arms slipped up around his neck, her fingers touching and tangling with his hair, brushing his ear, his chin. Her hands tingled with the joy of caressing him.

His mouth left hers then, and nibbled up the line of her cheek to her temple, her eyes. His tongue trailed over the thickly curling lashes, to teach her that every tiniest pore was a source of stinging electric charge, with lines that reached over her whole body.

She kissed his neck, breathing in the scent that was only him—masculine, heady, and pungent enough after his labours of the day to cut through every civilised barrier straight to her animal senses, with the urgent message of male potency.

His arms wrapped her safe against his chest, and he dropped backwards with her onto the mattress. She gasped in wild drunkenness, feeling the hard pressure of his body more fiercely now, and when his hand cupped her head and drew her face remorselessly down to his mouth, she seemed to melt again and again.

His lips devoured her with kisses. Every nerve in the world seemed attached to her lips, as if the sunset, the wind in the trees, the very evening chorus of the birds derived its inspiration from the movement of his mouth against her skin.

Her mouth could not get enough of him. Her hands held his head, her fingers threading and clenching through his curling black hair, desperate for more than kisses could give.

He knew it. His hand, caressing her, found the swell of her breast where it pressed against his chest, and trailed against it, and down over her back under the soft covering of her robe to her hips, and then up to press her back with delighting firmness.

Her body hungrily sought his, in little urgent pressings, and he lifted her head away from his kiss and smiled, shaking his head. Then he rolled her over onto her back, and lay above her on one elbow. His mouth lost its smile as his hand, free now to wander, ran hard up her outer thigh from knee to hip, with wild masculine possessiveness, as if defining his own territory.

She melted again with his hungry declaration of ownership, and when his hand pushed the silky slip up over her hip, as if he would not allow even that to trespass, she was assailed with such wild, desperate melting that she groaned.

She was another woman completely than the one she had been an hour ago. Nothing that she had believed and known about herself was real now. She hardly knew her name. All that was real about her was Jalal's hand, Jalal's body, his mouth, her need.

His mouth was against her breast, his tongue wetting

the silk to rub against her swollen hungry nipple. Shafts of delicious light exploded behind her eyelids, swept as sweet as honey to her skin, poured like celestial water through all her melting limbs.

A spiral of intensely burning fire spun hypnotically between her thighs, and her fingers clenched in his hair as she pulled her mouth from his to cry out. Dimly she realized that his hand was there on her sex, his fingers stroking the fiery spiral into being, stoking its urgency, on and on till her body, with shocking suddenness, began to clench spasmodically...then sensation and sweet delight etched new pathways of pleasure all through her, like water pouring along just-carved channels, bringing liquid delight to a starving, drought-stricken land, in a moment that went on to infinity.

"Oh!" was all she could say when it was over. Her body was flooded with heat and honey, and she lay feeling as lazy as a cat.

He bent and kissed her mouth, then lifted his head.

"We must go to my room now," he said.

She nodded dimly, her consciousness scarcely functioning. When he stood and reached a hand down for her, she obediently followed him to her feet.

He opened the door and glanced up and down the darkened hallway. A radio was playing softly somewhere.

"My room," she whispered. Her legs were like rubber. She had to concentrate to stand straight.

"All right," Jalal said. His mouth covered hers with a hungry, promising kiss. "Go there. I will follow in a moment."

She slipped along the passage and up the stairs to her own lair, amazed that she could still make her legs function. If they were hers. Her entire lower body felt melted. Her head was full of memories of what was just past, and at each one her body was swept with sensation that caused her knees to buckle.

In her attic room she swept clothes from a chair and tossed them into the closet, kicked shoes under the bed, fluffed pillows, straightened the already neat duvet. She turned on the lamp that was in the corner on the far side of the bed, and then stood looking down at the bed, cosily nested under the sloping roof, in its intimate circle of light, and heaved a sigh of anticipation that went all through her.

Ten

She heard light footsteps on the stairs, and chills raced up and down her being. She sat down on the bed, got up again, turned nervously as the door opened.

Jalal came through the door, pushed it silently shut, felt for the lock and turned the key with a grating sound that shot through her like a bolt of sensual lightning. He took a couple of steps towards her, enclosed her in one strong arm, and dropping something onto the bedside table, turned and wrapped her tightly to him, smothering her with the wildest kiss she had ever dreamed of, all her life long.

It went on forever, and it was all the kisses she had never had, it was a lifetime of kisses all in one. It was giving and taking, it was burning and ice, it was melting, utter, delicious delight.

When he lifted his head at last, she could only breathe his name.

''Take this off,'' he ordered softly, drawing her robe down over her shoulders and tossing it to one side.

She stood there trembling, with only the tiniest covering of silk between his hungry eyes and her body. Two narrow straps traced her perfectly formed shoulders. Thin turquoise silk, still damp from his mouth, caressed her warm, milky breasts, fell over swelling hips to brown, smooth thighs.

He bent his head, and his mouth settled just under her ear and trailed kisses down the side of her neck, while his hands enclosed her thighs with possessive firmness.

Just like that, she melted into flame.

His hand drew up the resistless silk, and with the lightest possible caress his fingers again brushed the warm, melting place where his body would soon demand entry.

Jalal understood that he had never been so lost in his life. Desire like the hot desert wind blasted him. She was every elemental force of nature against his being. He understood that all of nature's wildest forces, creative and destructive, that which brought both life and death, had one source, and that she took him there.

''My rose,'' he murmured, drowning in passion like a storm-swollen river in spring. He touched the rose and knew with the deepest, most primitive knowledge, that this part of her belonged to him. His to touch, to taste, to tantalize with his tongue and his body until the soft silk of the petals trembled and opened to him and willingly enclosed him.

Lightning streaked out from his fingertips and shot through all the wild hot colours of her being. Clio gasped, deep in her throat, and heard him grunt in response as if she had struck him, felt how his fiercely hard sex pulsed against her, heard the urgent, hungry whisper of his voice.

''Zahri,'' he whispered. ''Zahri.''

Zary.

Slowly the word penetrated the fog of pleasure that stupefied her. Clio gasped with shock. Splinters of ice rushed along her passion-swollen senses, cutting and slicing the softest parts of her being with a pain like nothing on earth.

She felt his touch now urging her down on the bed. He was murmuring in Arabic now, words of passion she didn't understand.

But she had understood enough.

"Let go of me!"

Like a drunkard, Jalal lifted his head and held her face between his two hands with bemused concern. "Clio?"

He seemed unaware that he had spoken any name but her own.

"Let *go!*"

He did not need to let go of her. She was already out of his hold, wrapping her arms over her beautiful breasts as if to protect herself from him.

"What is it, beloved?" he asked, frowning, unconsciously reaching for her again.

Stepping out of reach, she stared at him coldly for a moment, not answering. Her eyes were wide and black with such horror as he hoped never to see in a woman's eyes again. He swallowed.

"Clio! What is it? What—" And only then did he realize that he was not speaking English. "What is it?" he said again.

"Don't you ever touch me again," Clio said hoarsely. Blindly she groped for her robe, clutched it to her breasts, hiding herself from him.

"What has happened?" he cried softly. "What have you remembered?"

He stepped carefully towards her, sure that the solution lay within his own arms. "Tell me."

"God, I loathe men!" She stared at him, her chin up, as if it was himself that she hated, but he knew it could not be so. "Get out!"

"Clio," he said more urgently, as if his voice might bring sense to such blank wildness as he saw in her face.

She turned to the door, and under her hand the key scraped in the lock. Flinging open the door, she faced him again, a statue of anguish and fury.

"Get out!" she said again.

"I will go when you have told me what troubles you," he said, not moving from where he stood.

But she was lost in grief, anger, and violent self-loathing. She whirled and was out of the room before Jalal, master of the quick defence, could even engage his feet.

He did not follow her, but waited in the shadowed room, following with his ears as she stumbled down the stairs like a wounded animal.

He did not know, but thought he could guess, what made her run from such wild passion. There could not be more than one reason. Some man had hurt her. He had suspected it before, but now it was clear.

His heart tightened with the hardest, most bitter anger he had ever felt, like stone at the centre of his being, and he knew that if he met the man he would kill him, with one damning blow. There could be no mercy for a man who used his superior strength against a woman, when God had given him such strength to protect them.

He thought of her wild passion, remembered how she had opened her heart to him, then thought of the suddenness of her transformation.

What horror had she suddenly remembered, and why? What was the touch that was unbearable?

He felt that he wanted to heal the wound, to restore her to the full enjoyment of her passionate nature. He felt that he could do so. When he touched her, when she shivered, when she cried her pleasure, it was with a joy that was fresh, was new, and all this told him that other men had not been able to overcome her memories in the way that he had. She had allowed him to take her to unexplored places in herself....

He could teach her body, her spirit, a new memory. He could wipe out the old.

Clio pulled off her shorts and shirt to reveal a fashionable cream two-piece bathing suit, and stuffed them and her sandals into the waterproof bag, where her portable CD player, a novel, her towel and sun cream already were. In a separate bag she carried fresh fruit and a bottle of water.

All the residents of the Blake household, temporary and permanent, were expected to contribute labour according to their age, whether in the running of the house, or in the boutiques and marina. To the younger ones, of course, the "work" of observing how the cash register was operated, or a boat motor was repaired, often seemed more like play, especially when they were allowed to ring up a sale or insert a washer all by themselves.

There was a second iron-clad rule, too—they all took one day off each week. On that day they looked after only their own needs: they helped set the table or cook if they ate with the family, put their dishes in the dishwasher as usual, tidied away after games.

Sometimes in the busiest periods, of course, this rule went by the board for Maddy and Brandon and the older children; there were always rainy days when they could catch up. But today was Clio's scheduled day off, and unless all hell broke loose requiring her instant attendance, she was going to take it.

So after staying in bed late to avoid the family breakfast, and any meeting with Jalal, she had scribbled a note on the kitchen blackboard "Down at the cove, C"and slipped out.

Now, pausing a moment to clip her hair in place, she slipped into the deliciously cool water and, one hand clutching the waterproof bags, struck out for her favourite rock with a half sidestroke.

This small, out-of-the-way cove, only a twenty minute hike from home, had no beach, only a few precarious rocks at the bottom of the cliff. The water was deep right from the shore. At the mouth to the cove, a bed of reeds and a spread of rocks, some of them submerged, discouraged speedboats and jet-skis.

All this meant that in the mornings Clio could be pretty sure of being undisturbed, and, short of taking a boat to a more secluded beach, it was her favourite place to relax. And think.

And she had a lot to think of today, she told herself ironically, as she arrived at the large flat rock in the middle of the cove, dumped her things there, and slipped back into the welcoming water.

Well, what a glutton for punishment you are, she told herself with brutal self-contempt, as she dived deep under the surface into the rich, dark depths. Sunlight shafted down through the water, showing her her own greeny-white arms, and a startled fish made good its escape.

There must be something seriously wrong with her psyche. Twice in her life she'd been wildly attracted to a guy, and both times he just happened to be obsessed with her own sister? Just an unhappy coincidence?

Not very likely.

What weird and twisted mental wiring made her want to punish herself like this? Had she really felt so second-rate beside her gorgeous sister that she could only want a man who really wanted Zara?

Last night, she had looked back over the course of her life since that scarring moment with Peter and realized that many crucial conclusions about herself she had come to in those years were wrong. She was not a woman cursed with faint sexual appetites at all. She was a woman who had put herself in cold storage because of the hurt inflicted on her sexual image of herself at a critical, vulnerable moment—her first full sexual encounter.

Clio snorted, and the air bubbled like laughter through the water, but it was not lightness that she felt. Because what had it taken to show her this simple, obvious fact? How did she know it? Because her body was still running with a river of desperate, hungry sexual passion of a kind she had not felt since that night—had not, she saw now, *allowed* herself to feel since that night....

She surfaced, gasping for air, and floated for a time on her back, staring up at the hot sun.

Oh God, she was going to go out of her mind! How could she resist Jalal now, when the source of what she had been feeling for him, and had hidden under the convenient blankets of suspicion and hostility, was revealed in all its divine simplicity as pure, raw sexual attraction?

Yet how could she give in to it when she was facing another hurt identical to the first one?

Give me another one
Just like the other one...

She couldn't go through that again. Not with Jalal.

Well, at least this time she had had the courage and the sense to resist. She hadn't gone passive with Jalal as she had with Peter. She hadn't let him use her as a substitute for her own sister.

She squeezed her eyes shut, suddenly imagining how it would have been if he had not said her sister's name till later, till it was too late.... That would have been the end of the world.

If Jalal had made love to her wanting Zara, it would have killed her. Peter's betrayal had severed her access to her sex drive, but Jalal's—his would cut the cord to her heart.

She turned away from the thought, not wanting to see why that was so, and struck out in a hard, fast crawl.

But even that could not stop the hungry, coursing, melting desire that swept her body and soul every time she let herself whisper—*think!*—his name.

In the beautiful structure called for centuries past the King's Pavilion, three young men lay on cushioned divans, eating sweetmeats, with princely abandon. The Pavilion's broad walls of glass, at one end of a long, beautifully planned garden, overlooked a scene cool with fountains and serene with greenery.

It was one place of very few in the Barakat Emirates where the men—whose handsome faces would have been instantly recognizable to almost every one of their subjects—could be assured of complete privacy without anyone remarking the fact. By tradition guards prevented anyone entering the grounds that enclosed the Pavilion, whenever the monarch was in his refuge.

They could relax here, sure that no servant would trouble them unless rung for, that no subject would appear seeking a boon. And there was an additional factor that made the Pavilion a desirable place to be today.

It was swept for electronic bugs every day.

Even so, the princes—Karim, Omar and Rafi—took the added precaution of sitting by one of the small inside fountains, for the sound of running water confuses voice-transmitting devices.

They were handsomely negligent, lying in the cool, traditional summer costume of baggy white cotton trousers, their chests bare under open shirts, their feet and dark heads also bare. They appeared totally relaxed. No one could have suspected, seeing their casual postures, that what they discussed now was a heavy matter of state.

"He has been approached," Prince Karim was saying, for the King's Pavilion was in the gardens of his own palace, on the shores of the Gulf of Barakat, and it was he who had received the news.

They were all silent for a moment, absorbing this evidence of the truth of their suspicions.

Prince Omar's eyebrows went up as he thoughtfully took it in. "I suppose that's good," he said at last. Absently he reached for the lid of a polished gold humidor, lifted it and drew out one of his favourite small cigars.

"Any hint yet who by?" Prince Rafi asked.

"None."

They all waited as Omar carefully lit his cigar. Rafi took up two walnuts, cracked one against the other, and dropped the whole one back in the plate.

"And how did he respond?" Omar drawled, absently

watching the end of his cigar, as if the smoke might scribble the truth they sought in the air before his eyes.

"He'd be a fool to show interest so soon," Rafi said, tossing the meat of the walnut into his mouth.

Karim nodded. "And they would scarcely wish to work with a fool."

"They may wish soon enough that he was one," said Omar, with a dry smile. "I wonder why it does not occur to such intriguers that once installed in power he would have no more need of their assistance."

"Perhaps they feel that they will not need *him* for long," Rafi suggested.

"I wonder if you're right. Will they offer guarantees?"

"If they are wise," insisted Omar dryly, "they will *ask* for them."

Eleven

"Clio."

Oblivious to any outside sound, she lay stretched on the warm, flat rock, her earphones in her ears, drowning her worries with fem-rock music at a volume just below permanent damage level.

"Clio."

Her skin was smooth, brown, glistening with sweat and sun cream. Her long loose hair fell down over the edge of the low rock, its tips just trailing in the water. A couple of minnows were nipping curiously at them. One arm was stretched languidly out, hanging over the water, the palm half cupped with lazy vulnerability.

If he heaved out of the water and lay between her thighs and kissed her, would she resist?

He suppressed the impulse, staying in the water and watching the long lines of leg and hip, the generous curve of her breasts above the white material of her suit, the full glistening lips, the curl of her eyelashes.

She appealed to him as no other woman had ever done. He would require every ounce of discipline he possessed to control his need and subdue it to her own need, go at her pace.

Rather than try to compete with the angry music blasting into her ears, he lifted an arm from the water and sent a light spray across the neatly muscled expanse of her abdomen.

She blinked and turned her head, after a few moments finding him against the sun. Then one hand groped to the CD player and killed the sound, the other meanwhile drawing the earphones from her ears.

Then they were still for an unmeasured moment, gazing into each other's eyes as the sun beat down and the water lapped and paradise seemed to beckon.

Seeing the note she had left, he had followed her here, where they might be private, and where, away from her family, she might be encouraged to tell him a little of the history that had scarred her. But when he looked at her, those searching dark eyes, that generous mouth—all speech seemed to dry in his throat.

Clio gazed at him, and almost cried out with the surge of conflicting sensations—melting in her body, anguish in her heart. Her entire body seemed turned to liquid sugar, sweet, warm, delicious. Just seeing him, like a seal beside her in the water, his head lifted to stare at her…she sensed the elemental self of him. He was like a creature still more than half-wild, and that knowledge thrilled her.

He was pursuing her for reasons all his own, and that stifled her breath.

He heaved himself half out of the water onto the rock beside her, but there was not enough room for two on her rock, unless he lay so close that lovemaking became inevitable.

It was already intimate enough, his body propped on his elbows, his shoulders above her.... The posture of his body, and her own, invited him to sink down and kiss her.

She rolled and sat up abruptly, turning away from him, dragging her bag over and thrusting the CD player into it. Her back shivered with the nearness of his heat.

"What do you want, Jalal?" she asked coolly over her shoulder as he pulled himself up to a sitting position behind her.

Her skin was so warmly brown against the white of her swimsuit. He knew many Arab men who longed for pale, blonde women, but he had never felt the draw. For him, as for the ancient poets and storytellers, it was dark eyes and hair that caused the heart to beat uncomfortably fast....

"To be with you." He stopped, coughed, and breathed deep.

Suddenly he realized the impossibility of broaching such a subject with words. What could he tell her? *I can be patient while we slay the demons that haunt you?* Would she be angered if he told her to what conclusions he had jumped?

And suppose he was wrong? Perhaps he had merely convinced himself of the truth of his suspicions to hide the hurt another interpretation of last night's events would deliver to his male ego? Suppose it was himself she objected to, and not to the act at all?

No. He had seen her eyes. And it was not him that she had seen when horror gripped her.

"I guess it never occurred to you that you are the last person in the world I want to be with right now," she observed in a conversational tone.

"Yes, it occurred to me. But I thought, too, that if we talked about last night a little, you might change your mind."

Her heart shrivelled. God in Heaven, why didn't he have the sense to shut up? What on earth did he imagine he could possibly say to make anything better?

It didn't help that the incantation *It's Zara you want* was about as effective as sunglasses against a supernova. When she looked at him, felt him there, she still burned to touch him. Her body was on fire and aching for him. No matter what she knew.

Not like Peter at all. When she had seen Peter again, when he had tried to touch her, assuring her that after all he really was attracted to her for herself, her stomach had heaved with disgust.

So, did this constitute progress? Clio asked herself with bitter humour. She let out a choked laugh at the thought.

"Do you know," she informed him brightly, "I really don't want to hear anything at all about last night!"

She had been hurt, and he knew he could heal her. He was as sure as he could be that he could get behind whatever was making her say these things…and maybe she knew it, too, in some part of herself, and wanted to be released….

"Can we not say a little?" She was stonily silent, her back rigid and turned against him.

"I came here because I wanted to be alone."

"Sometimes, is it not better not to be alone, even though in a part of yourself, you wish it?"

"I am not a damsel in distress, Jalal. I am not a kitten up a tree."

He paused. "I do not understand these cultural idioms," he observed, with a tone that forced a laugh from her.

He swallowed and rubbed his chin.

"Such a hot day!" he murmured. "Why did no one warn me that in summer Canada, the land of ice and snow, is as hot as spring in the desert?"

"It's a closely guarded secret," she said, without expression. "Otherwise half the millionaires in the world would want to buy property here and force the prices up."

She knew she was just at the edge of control. She was trembling inwardly, and she could feel the tears threatening from deep in her being.

She began hastily packing up her things, shoving her towel and book into her bag, picking up the bag half filled with strawberries.

"Clio, don't leave," he said.

"Jalal, what happened happened. I think we both have to agree that it will be better if it never happens again."

She sounded angry, but underneath, he knew, she was only hurt. He did not know how he knew it. By some magic between them, that had never happened to him before, telling him her inmost thoughts and feelings.

If he could touch her, take her in his arms, if he could hold and comfort her, she would tell him what past hurt had made her react in this way. But he must be careful. Until he knew more of what had caused her change last night, any physical move on his part might reignite the memories....

"No. I do not agree. I think we should not be put off by what happened."

He knew that it was important to tell her that he had not been angered by her abrupt rejection of him in the heat of the moment. She had to know that he was capable of controlling himself, of accepting with patience whatever she needed.

She almost laughed at the sheer ludicrousness of that. What was he going to say? That he would be happy to accept her as a Zara substitute if she didn't object? That the price for the hottest sexual pleasure she would ever experience was to let him imagine he was with her sister?

Well, fortunately she had been down that road before. She knew the trip wasn't worth it.

"Do you!" she said, with a cynical half laugh. "Well, no doubt I'm turning down an opportunity in a million, but you'll have to excuse me."

"Clio…" he begged.

She should jump into the water and leave him. But she felt bound to him by the cords of electric feeling that swept her body at his nearness. She wanted to reach for him, to touch the source of the pleasure that swept her. Like smelling your favourite, deliciously cooked food, she thought in a ridiculous aside, and wanting a taste….

If she turned to him now she would get more than a taste. She would get the full-course meal, and nothing she could tell herself would stop her wanting it from him. She was on a knife-edge and she knew it. She was shivering with years of pent-up need.

But if she gave in to this crazy desire to throw herself against Jalal's muscled, water-beaded chest, be wrapped in his willing arms—she would risk another deeply soul-destroying experience.

"Jalal, I don't want to hear it!" she said. Then, exerting all her self-discipline, she grabbed up the waterproof bags and slid into the water.

Out of her paranoia, she began to watch him. He would speak on the phone to someone, in Arabic, his voice soft as if he were afraid of being overheard, even here, where no one understood the language. On his time off, he took a boat and disappeared, sometimes for hours.

Once, driving past in a boat, she saw him on a restaurant dock, sitting with two dark men, and she was sure they were the same two who had hired the boat that day, and refused to let Ben go along.

She remembered that moment, on the day he arrived, when he had forgotten his stated reasons for coming here. She had reminded him that he was here to practise his English. "Yes," he'd said, but she remembered that she had wondered, and she began to wonder again now, what his real reasons were.

He knew he was a fool if he blamed her attitude entirely on some other man's actions. He had to look into himself for the cause of Clio's repudiation of him. It was too easy to attribute her behaviour entirely to past trauma.

He had to accept that she also blamed him, believed him capable of the kind of behaviour that had caused her own evil memories.

For the first time, he began seriously to wonder whether more than he understood had happened to Zara while he held her hostage. Always before he had believed that his word was law with his men. Had one of them defied the ban he had imposed?

Surely his mother would have known, even if he himself did not, a part of him argued. And if his mother had known, she would certainly have told him. She, who had always disapproved of his plans in the strongest terms, who had bitterly reviled him when she learned that he had returned to camp with Prince Rafi's intended wife as his captive, had visited Zara twice every day. She could have had no hesitation in telling him if, as a result of his arrogant stupidity, his hostage had been hurt.

Unless… He thought of his mother's history, and his grandmother's. Both of them had suffered because of the archaic attitude that said a woman who lost her virginity before marriage, whether she was at fault or not, could be written out of history, even killed.

Nusaybah, his mother, had escaped death at her own father's hands because, and only because, the illegitimate child she carried in her womb was the grandchild of a king who no longer had an heir. She had been forced into marriage, with a man old enough to be her grandfather, to save her reputation in the tribe.

Jalal gasped, making a connection for the first time. But she must have been still in love with Prince Aziz! In love with a handsome prince, mourning his death, carrying his son, and forced to marry that old man…

And no doubt, Jalal saw suddenly, she had had to put up with whatever her husband exacted from her in return for the favour of his protection.

These were things his mother had never spoken of. But the tribe had never been kind to women. Women were better off in the cities of Barakat, where a secular state imposed its own codes.

His grandmother, Nusaybah's mother, a princess, had also suffered deeply. Abandoned to her fate, with no choice but to marry the bandit who had abducted and raped her—or flee into the desert and die.

She had survived on memories of her old life, its cool water and green trees, until a mercifully early death.

Had these facts surfaced in his mother's mind? Had she moved to protect the hostage by denying that such a thing had ever happened, in order to, as she might well believe, save Zara's life—or at the very least, her marriage to the prince?

If so, and if he knew it, Rafi would by now have killed

the man. Nor would he have allowed Jalal himself to be treated as he was now being treated, trusted as he was now trusted, by his uncles.

So if it had happened, Zara had not told Rafi.

But might she have confided in her sister?

Perhaps even, it had occurred in darkness, so that Zara had not known who it was, had believed he himself was her attacker?

There was more to Clio's abrupt rejection of him than the scars of the past. He must find out his own share of her trouble.

"Are you watched?"

"Of course I am watched! We are undoubtedly under observation at this moment," Jalal said impatiently. "Can you not at least attempt to disguise yourselves in the local costume?"

The men looked down at their own neat suits and pale tailored shirts in surprise. "Is this not—?" one began.

"You are not in the city now! Here the traditional dress is such as you see me wearing."

They looked at his brightly patterned, baggy shorts, his cotton shirt open over a white T-shirt, and nodded. "Your point is noted, Excellency."

"You might also try to look as if you are here to fish."

"Of course," they said, and then glanced uncertainly at each other, wondering how to do it. He almost laughed.

"Here's a worm. Bait the hook."

The worm wriggled. The dark man withdrew his hand. "This worm is alive."

Jalal glanced at him with a coldness in his eyes that made the other feel how close the grave might be. "You involve yourself in plots that will result in the deaths of thousands and you cringe at a worm? Of course the worm is alive," he said. "That is how the fish like them."

Twelve

——

"Clio, I ask you to tell me something," Jalal began without preamble, grabbing the first opportunity in days. It was pouring with rain outside. The children had been taken by their parents to see a famous visiting circus in a town miles away, leaving the two of them in charge. At lunchtime he had left the hired help alone in the mostly deserted marina and come to the house.

"Even if Zara has sworn you to strict secrecy, you must now find a way to tell me the truth. Who among my men hurt your sister when she was in my…"

"Prison?" Clio supplied brightly. She busied herself with the sandwich she was making, keeping her back to him. She had not conquered her physical reaction to him. Bad enough when they were merely in the same room together. When he focussed his attention on her she could hardly keep her knees from buckling.

"Yes," he agreed softly. "In my prison. Did she suffer more than I knew?"

She turned, summoning her old anger as her shield against present feelings. "You know, it's fascinating," she observed. "You talk as if Zara was the only one who could have suffered anything because of you. Do you have any idea, Jalal, what hell we went through here, knowing some rebel fanatic with a score to settle had taken Zara hostage thousands of miles away? Can you conjure up the glimmer of an idea of what my mother and father went through?"

"Yes, of course, I—"

"No," she contradicted flatly. "No, because if you did, you would never have come here." Oh, how she wished he had not! "You would never have so blithely expected them to play host to you after what you had done to us all. You thought that because Zara survived more or less unscathed and you very kindly didn't let your men have a regular go at her, the way we all feared for days on end, that it was all over and no harm done.

"Let me fill you in—my father was as grey as death from the moment we got the news Zara had been abducted to the moment he heard her voice on the phone telling him she was fine. I thought he was going to have a heart attack, and no doubt he would have, if it had gone on much longer. I was terrified it was going to kill them both.

"And the kids, too. Even Donnelly. We couldn't keep it from the kids. Everyone in the country knew about it— it was on television twenty-four hours a day! They called her the Barakat Hostage, did you know that? It was 'Day Three in the Barakat Hostage Crisis' for the journalists, but for us it was another twenty-four hours, one thousand four hundred and forty minutes, of fear, misery, and feelings so horrible I bet you've never experienced anything like it in your life.''

He was silent, listening.

''All right, I accept that nothing worse than the fact of imprisonment happened to her. But don't think that knowing that wipes away all the scars, Jalal. You don't recover from an experience like that just because it's all over now.''

She was reminding herself as she spoke, and the old feelings now poured up through the well hole she had at last created, and flooded her.

A hundred protests rose to his lips and were quelled as she spoke. He forced himself to listen, not to defend himself in word or thought, but to let what she said find its mark in his heart.

He listened as she ran out of words and began to weep, and he did not make the mistake of trying to touch her when she did. How could he offer himself as her comforter when the wounds she described had been inflicted by himself?

When all the words and all the storm of weeping were finished he sat in silence with her. She wiped her nose and face, letting the sobs subside. Finally she raised her head and looked at him.

''Thank you,'' he said then. ''Thank you for telling me what I did not understand before. I have heard what you said, Clio.''

She had not told him everything. She had not said anything about the fact that he had fallen for her sister and then tried to exorcise his illicit passion for his uncle's wife on her own sister's body. She had not said that she wondered how deep his love for Zara went, and whether he was willing to betray Prince Rafi in order to gain her.

* * *

''Rest assured, your uncles will not be martyrs.''

It was a hot, sunny day. Two men sat at a table on the terrace of the rented mansion overlooking the lake. Below, beside a small yacht, Jalal's boat bobbed on the swell caused by a passing speedboat. A serving man silently set tiny cups of strong coffee and a plate of honeyed cakes down in front of them and silently withdrew.

Saifuddin ar Ratib was the name of the man who had spoken. He had replaced Abu Abdullah in the negotiations. He was more intelligent, more powerful, closer to the heart of the conspiracy…more dangerous.

''I have not the pleasure of understanding you,'' said Jalal.

''Considering the lives they lead, each might easily expire in circumstances that are sure to disgust true believers.''

Abruptly Jalal lost interest in the coffee he was stirring. He set the spoon into the saucer and looked up at this latest emissary from whoever it was.

''How so?'' he demanded softly.

Saifuddin ar Ratib raised an eyebrow. They had him. He himself had seen the light of greed in the prince's eyes, however Jalal had tried to feign lack of interest.

''A fatal car accident at the moment when a prince is being serviced by a cheap whore—or perhaps two— would leave little for the people to regret in the passing of such a libertine.''

''And which of my uncles has a taste for such pursuits?''

The man, whose name meant ''The Arranger'' and was undoubtedly a pseudonym, shrugged largely and showed his palms.

''This is merely an example of what might possibly

happen to the kind of man who would make a foreign unbeliever queen of an honourable and believing people.''

Jalal lifted an eyebrow. ''Have not all my uncles' brides accepted the faith?''

''Lip service merely. It is a known fact that at least one of them encourages the prince to drink alcohol.''

''If you mean Omar, I doubt if he caught his taste for Scotch from his wife.''

''Nevertheless, if he killed himself and her in an accident caused by his own drunkenness, who would mourn?''

There was a silence broken by the drone of boats, the slap of water against the dock. Jalal got to his feet and walked to the railing. He stood looking out over the water, then turned.

''Do your friends indeed have their plans so carefully constructed already?'' Jalal asked quietly.

Saifuddin ar Ratib's hand went up pacifically. ''Rest assured, Prince, I give you no more than possibilities. Nothing would be firmly planned or executed without your approval.''

''Good.'' Prince Jalal ibn Aziz showed his teeth. ''Take this back to those who sent you—let them not forget that I am bound by my grandfather's deathbed command, and subject to his curse. To send the princes into exile, to reunite the divided country and take the throne in their place—this would be perhaps no more than is my right. Although of course I do not say so.''

''Of course.'' Saifuddin ar Ratib nodded blandly.

''To allow them to be assassinated is so far from possible, that I would be on my honour to hunt down the perpetrators of such crimes, from the lowly doers to the highest planners, to kill them and all their kin without mercy. I would spread their blood on the desert sands and wipe their line from the face of the earth forever.''

Saifuddin smiled, his good humour unabated. ''Prince, do you indeed live in terror of an old man's fantasies?'' He lifted his hands. ''A curse? Are you not an educated man?''

Jalal inclined his head. ''But my people—my uncles' people,'' Jalal corrected himself quickly, ''are not. If I did not obey King Daud's injunctions, the entire country would expect to see me dethroned, and every petty sheikh in the desert would think it worth his while to challenge my rule.''

Saifuddin nodded. ''I take your point. But—is it not worth the risk? In exile, would not the three princes form an even more potent rallying point for the disaffected?''

Jalal stood and looked arrogantly down as if Saifuddin ar Ratib were an insect he might crush.

''I am Jalal ibn Aziz ibn Daud ibn Hassan al Quraishi,'' he said. ''That will be enough for the people.''

She was a strong woman.

He thought of the woman named Nusaybah—his mother's namesake—one of the Prophet's earliest disciples. At the battle of Uhud, when it had gone so badly for his army, the Prophet had been under direct attack with only a small group to defend him. Nusaybah had been one of that group. She was armed, with the Prophet's express permission, and she stood in front of the Prophet that day and defended his life.

''The Prophet himself allowed women to be different,'' Jalal's mother had said, when she recited this story to him. ''He was a great warrior himself, but he allowed a woman to defend his life. You also, my son, be a man who is not afraid when a woman is strong.''

Like his mother, much of Clio's strength was in her moral judgements. Sometimes a woman's moral strength was harder to accept than the physical. He could no longer reject her condemnation of him.

He had to face the fact that, like any criminal, he had used his superior strength against a woman, for his own ends. He had held himself above such men, believing that because his own ends were political, he remained morally unstained by his actions.

He was wrong. But how to tell her what he had learned?

Clio wandered through the days in a haze of dullness, punctuated by sharp spear thrusts of humiliating memory.

Now she could understand so much that she had never understood before. Now she could see the long line of underground motivation that had been driving her ever since that long-ago night with Peter Clifford, and had led her straight to this situation with Jalal.

When Peter had gone on to make love to her that night, after calling Zara's name—her body had responded. That was what she had wanted to forget. That was what she couldn't bear to face. In spite of what she knew, she had thrilled when he stroked her. She had moaned when he moved in her, in spite of the first-time pain, had arced her body hungrily to meet the thrust of his....

And she had despised herself afterwards. How could she have let him do that to her, when in his imagination he was with Zara?

It had been the rape of her own soul. And she had acquiesced in it.

From that moment, Clio saw, she had considered her body the enemy. Something that had to be ruthlessly controlled. She had suppressed her sexual nature ruthlessly, without even being aware that she did so. She had not allowed any man to create more than the mildest response in her. She was always in control.

Jalal had threatened that facade. Because her sexual and emotional response to him was more powerful than anything she had experienced before, she had unconsciously realized that he was a profound threat to her self-control.

She thought of the moment when he had stepped into the boat and fallen, remembered how strong her reaction had been, how swiftly her defences had moved to deny it…. That had set the pattern for everything that had happened since.

She had pretended to herself that what she felt was righteous anger, and because she had a long history of suppressing and disguising her sexual nature, she had been pretty successful at the deception—until the day she had stood outside the door listening to him with Rosalie. As though it was only by plumbing the deepest well of suspicion that she could let go of everything else…like a door that you have to push further shut in order to unhook the latch and open it.

How richly tangled the human psyche was! Clio found time to marvel detachedly.

But turning the microscope of real understanding on herself was not an easy task. She was alternately burning and freezing with self-condemnation and contempt. Because even if she had invented the brutality of his nature…she had not invented his attraction to Zara.

She must have unconsciously picked that up from him right at the beginning. The messages must have been there. It was nothing but more self-deception if she tried to pretend now that she could not have known it, that it was merely coincidence that she had fallen for yet another man who wanted not her but Zara.

What horrid little twist of her psychological makeup dictated that she could be deeply sexually aroused only by men who really wanted Zara?

God, she needed a shrink! What had driven her to repeat that horrific experience, the worst and most crippling encounter of her life? What was wrong with her?

Every Friday night in the season, Maddy Blake drew up a duty roster for the coming week. Mostly this was for the sake of the younger children, who enjoyed the whole process of negotiation, and were learning something about duty and responsibility. Even Donnelly knew that when she was scheduled for half an hour in the ice cream shop she had to be there, and felt her importance in the scheme of things.

Each of the Blake children had learned to consult the schedule for their own "plaque" from a time before they could read.

Donnelly's sign, carefully chosen by herself, was a butterfly. In the same way, nearly twenty years ago, Clio had chosen the picture of a black-and-white cat. The boys usually went for something more macho—Ben was a Jedi knight, Jonah a shark.

Part of the ritual that introduced any new member, however temporary, to this household was the choosing of the plaque that would, for the length of their stay, be used to signify them on the duty roster.

"Okay, Harry is going to be staying for a while, I take it?" Brandon would ask at the family breakfast.

The prospective tenant would nod eagerly.

"Has someone explained the house rules?"

More nods.

"Do you agree to abide by the rules as outlined to you, Harry?" Brandon would pursue gravely.

"Yes, Uncle Brandon." One of the rules was that you called Brandon *Uncle* and Maddy *Aunt,* unless you preferred to call them *sir* and *ma'am.*

"All right, and have you chosen a plaque, Harry?"

"I picked the Chief on the horse."

Clio rarely needed to consult the roster—which took the form of a board on the kitchen wall full of little metal cup hooks on which the plaques were hung in rows—because these days her duties were nearly always the same. She generally supervised between the craft boutique and the ice cream shop, while her mother ran the gallery and supervised "The Barn."

Clio's schedule was different on Saturdays, when she and Ben together made the rounds of all the rental cottages, changing sheets and towels and checking to see that everything had been left clean and in order before the new renters came in the afternoon.

So she didn't even eyeball the roster until Saturday morning at ten, when she was in the kitchen with all the linens, waiting for Ben to make his appearance. Absently spooning yogurt into her mouth, she paused in front of the big board with its display of plaques that had been a part of her summers all her life long.

Her father's plaque, a guitar because he still often played while they sang together on long winter evenings, almost always had the picture of the sailboat under it, which of course signified the marina. What was under her mother's rose, though, had changed over the years. When Clio was tiny, there had been first only an ice cream, and then a paintbrush, but now there were added to the repertoire a tiny Mountie, to signify the crafts boutique, and a farmer with a pitchfork, who symbolized the pioneer barn.

The arrangement was a source of security to them all.

Even those too young to read need only consult this chart to learn exactly where their parents were.

Cottage duty was signified by a tiny house with a smoking chimney, and there it was as usual under Clio's cat. She blinked absently, swallowing another spoonful. Under the Jedi there was no matching house. Ben was apparently on marina duty this morning.

Then who was coming to do the cottages with her?

Frowning over this little mystery, Clio searched the board for another house plaque. And then she found it…under the tiger.

Thirteen

He's a very wild tiger!

Chills rushed all over her skin. *Jalal* was coming on the cottage run with her? Why on earth would her mother have arranged this?

Jalal stage-managed it! she told herself fiercely and, setting the yogurt container on the counter so hurriedly that it slipped and fell, spilling its contents on the floor, turned and ran. Out of the kitchen and down the hall to the front door, out and along the pretty, tree-lined street under the picturesquely lowering sky, over the bridge, till she arrived panting at the art gallery, in a beautiful century-old red brick building.

"Mother!" she cried, storming in. In spite of the heavily overcast sky, two middle-aged women in poplin shorts and blouses were in the main gallery, standing in front of a massive canvas of a mountain disguised as a sleeping woman. They turned to gaze at her.

Behind the desk, her mother put down her pen and looked up.

"What's wrong, Clio?" she asked impassively. Clio was dramatic by nature, and the stormy entry made less impression on Maddy than on the tourists.

Embarrassed by the two women's attention, she rushed over to the desk. "Why is Jalal down for cottage duty this morning?" she hissed.

"Weren't you there? Oh no, that's right, you were out last night." Clio had been to a friend's birthday party, where they had driven her crazy demanding to know what it was like living with a prince….

She couldn't escape him.

"The people in Solitaire called to say the generator had practically given up altogether. Jalal agreed to go this morning and see if it could be fixed."

"What does *Jalal* know about fixing generators?" Clio demanded in stagey disbelief.

Maddy gave her the benefit of raised eyebrows. "Quite a bit, apparently. He did after all run that camp of his on wind and a prayer most of the time, you know."

"I'll just bet! Well, I don't want him along! Can't Dad come?"

"Your father wants to be in the marina this morning. He asked Jalal to do it. Why is it a problem, Clio?" Maddy regarded her severely over the top of her reading glasses. "Apart from the fact that you refuse to overcome your dislike of him."

"Because I—" Where to start? Clio wondered hopelessly. "I just don't want to spend the day with him. He'll probably leave me to make the beds by myself in some kind of macho—"

Her mother gazed at her with disapproval. "I think you know that's unjust. However, if you feel that strongly about it, I don't see why Rosalie can't take your place."

"Rosalie!"

"If you think she knows the ropes sufficiently."

"But I—Rosalie can't..."

"Clio, I have customers here. Please sort it out yourself. Whatever you think is best," said Maddy.

She turned away to speak to one of the tourist women who had approached the desk. "Yes, sorry, do you have a question?"

"That's all right," said the woman comfortably. "Would you have any inexpensive prints by Jerry Eagle Feather?"

"I have a couple of limited edition prints—oh, excuse me a moment! Clio!" her mother cried as she got to the door.

She turned.

"If Rosalie does go, remind her to keep an eye out for the Williamses' cat at Solitaire."

Nodding, Clio went back out onto the street. That was how important it all was to her mother. Either she or Rosalie had to spend the next few hours alone with Jalal, and uppermost in her mother's mind was the Williamses' missing cat!

Clio jogged back to the house. In the kitchen she found Jalal standing by the back door, a cup of coffee in his hand, staring out at the darkly brooding sky that only enhanced her mood.

"There is going to be a storm, I think," he said.

She laughed nervously. "Yeah, probably."

"The boat is loaded. Are you ready to go?"

She stood uncertainly in the middle of the room, gazing blindly at him, feeling her skin already twitching with awareness. "Ummm...yeah," she said, trying to think. Should she ask Rosalie to do it? "Yeah, I guess so."

She glanced up at the duty board, found Rosalie's

plaque. Working in the Barn this morning. Rosalie loved it there, being with all the artisans…still, she would happily trade that in for a day spent with Jalal.

What if Rosalie used the opportunity to make a sexual move on Jalal? What if he made love to *her* and called Zara's name? Did he understand that fifteen-year-olds were jailbait in this country?

Jalal moved to the sink, putting down his empty coffee cup. Someone had cleaned up the yogurt she had dropped.

"Shall we go?" he asked, holding open the screen door.

His face was a tight mask of anger, as if he knew exactly what she was thinking about.

Feeling that her brain still wasn't working, Clio followed him out.

"Is the line completely secure?" asked Rafi.

Karim, bent over the keyboard, nodded. "Yes, we have the highest security encryption. Wait a minute, here we go."

A tense silence fell as the three princes bent to the computer monitor. With slow stripes down the screen an image was forming.

"Pretty good," Omar observed. "How far away was the camera?"

"This is from Ramiz. He was positioned in a fishing boat perhaps a few hundred yards away."

There was silence as the princes waited. Suddenly the image gelled. "That is Jalal?" said Omar, his finger pointing to a man whose back was to the camera. Over his shoulder another man's face gazed almost directly into the camera.

"That is Jalal," Rafi agreed. "Who is the other?"

They were silent, frowning with concentration. "I have seen this face before," Omar said.

"Yes," Karim breathed. "So have I. But who is it?"

"What name does he use?"

"Saifuddin ar Ratib."

Rafi shook his head. *"Sword of the Faith, The Arranger."* He murmured the translation thoughtfully. "A nom de guerre, obviously."

"Perhaps Akram got some better shots. Pull up some more."

Karim punched the keyboard. "But the face is clear enough. It is just that—the circumstances are missing."

"The man's head is bare," Omar said suddenly. "It could be we are more used to seeing him with a *keffiyeh*."

"Yes," said Karim slowly, as another photo began to form. "Yes."

Jalal slowed the engine and guided the boat into Bent Needle River.

Renters had to vacate the cottages by ten on Saturday morning, and the incoming ones couldn't take possession till five in the afternoon. That arrangement usually gave Clio more than enough time to do what was needed to put the cottages in shape for the new arrivals.

But a faulty generator was an unknown quantity. Maybe it could be fixed on site, with the tools he brought with him, or maybe not. It might need a new part, which would mean a trip back to the marina and out again, in which case he would probably still be working on it when the renters arrived.

Clio and Jalal had gone through the work at all the other cottages as fast as possible, leaving Solitaire till last. They had hardly spoken all morning, except for what was absolutely required to get the work done.

She was nervous and jittery in his company, and it was harder to disguise than she would have guessed. Making the beds was the worst trial. Even with the space of a bed between them, his powerful aura seemed to affect her with longing and anguish. Or maybe it was *because* it was the space of a bed between them…

She knew he knew. But he said nothing. If she stiffened when his hand came too close, he did not make it obvious that he knew, but nevertheless withdrew his hand instantly.

He was careful not to brush up against her, always waiting till she left any room first….

After a while the embarrassment she felt at making her uncontrollable sexual awareness so obvious was adding acutely to her discomfort. Thank God he would have something else to do at Solitaire!

She glanced at her watch as they rounded the bend and the dock came in sight.

"Oh!" she remembered suddenly. "Will you keep your eye out for a cat while we're here?"

"A cat?" he repeated.

"A couple of weeks ago the Williamses were here with their cat, and it went missing. They had to leave without it. We've been leaving dry food out, which gets eaten—but that could be raccoons, of course. The Williamses are very upset. They call every second day, but none of the renters have seen anything so far."

"What colour is the cat?" he asked with a lazy smile.

"Black and white." She laughed at a sudden thought. "For goodness' sake, Jalal, don't go grabbing any skunks! If it's sporting a wide white stripe down the middle of its back, you leave it alone!"

He looked at her. "I don't intend to grab any black-

and-white cat, either. It will have to come to me of its own accord.''

She suspected him of double meaning, and her cheeks got hot. What was he suggesting? That if she wanted him she would have to make the first move?

That was just fine with her. She had no intention of exploring her newfound sexual self with him, one way or the other. She wouldn't be making any moves on him, and it was a relief to hear this declaration that he wouldn't be making any on her.

She wasn't naive enough to think that just because Jalal was maybe in love with Zara he wasn't actually attracted to Clio for her own sake, too. At sixteen, she had believed that kind of thing, but now she knew better. For men sexual attraction was a pretty random response. Of course he was capable of making love to Clio even if his heart was elsewhere. Men did that all the time, didn't they? Even men who could have the one woman they loved cheated.

And one thing had to be said in his behalf—at least the woman he really wanted was absolutely forbidden to him. He could hardly be expected to swear himself to chastity for the sake of another man's wife.

Looking at it rationally, Jalal really hadn't done anything *criminal*. It was just their mutual bad luck that the woman whose name he had murmured was Clio's sister, and that the incident held such deep and distressing memories for her.

Probably, like Peter, he would never figure out why a little slip like the wrong name in the heat of the moment bothered her so much. If he even realized it had escaped him. If he didn't, he probably figured she was a complete neurotic.

It was a huge relief to know he wouldn't be trying anything.

Thunder rumbled threateningly as he guided the boat in, and a sudden wind warned them that the rain was on top of them. Clio jumped onto the dock with the bow line. Heavy drops began to fall as Jalal off-loaded the plastic bag of linens and the toolbag.

On the verandah, she fished the keys out of her pocket. "I'll do the housework by myself, Jalal, if you want to get started on the generator."

He nodded as she pushed the door open. "Will you be all right on your own?"

He meant, because of what had happened last time they were here together. But she had been back every Saturday since that incident, and Solitaire was too lovely for bad associations to cling.

Still, on those other occasions, she hadn't gone inside alone. Ben had been with her.

"Would you mind just coming in with me first?" she asked.

Leaving his toolbag on the verandah, he stepped inside after her, and together they walked through the place. He was careful not to follow her through a doorway too closely.

But that only drew attention to the fact that they were completely isolated here.

Solitaire wasn't very big, only two bedrooms, but it was in a beautiful location. This cottage always got repeat customers.

Honeymooners in particular loved it. Several couples, having come for the first time on their honeymoon, came back year after year. The site was both sunny and secluded, with lots of mature deciduous trees. And you couldn't get more private.

The big L-shaped dining/sitting room was filled with dappled light throughout the day, though not on a day like today. Today it felt cosy and protected from the coming storm.

The master bedroom was beautifully decorated, and had a king-size bed....

When they had walked through the place together and found everything in order, Jalal picked up his tools again and went off through the rain to the small shed among the trees.

From one of the bedroom windows Clio watched him go, her heart thumping. He was so gorgeous. The way he moved, as if he'd been walking these forests for centuries! It appealed to something in her so deep it seemed to hurt her heart.

She noticed he didn't duck his head, or run, to avoid the rain. He seemed to like walking through rainfall. No, it wasn't quite that. He *accepted* the rain—in the same way as he accepted the earth under his feet, the tree branches that brushed his shoulders.

She watched, sighing, till he was out of sight among the trees.

She worked at an easy pace, while wind and rain began to slap at the windows. After absent-mindedly flicking the sitting-room lamp a few times, she realized she couldn't put the lights on with the generator down, and she worked in the grey half-light, dusting and polishing, stripping the beds and making them with fresh sheets, cleaning the bathroom and kitchen, laying out fresh towels.

And thought of Jalal.

I don't intend to grab any black-and-white cat. It will have to come to me of its own accord.

She supposed she would be forever grateful to him, once she got over the agony of repeating trauma. Whatever else he had done, he had shown her that she was a woman with a normal sex drive, and had given her back the promise of a fulfilled life.

Not with him, of course. And probably never again with the powerful passion she felt right now. Her feelings and emotions were so deeply aroused that she felt they could kill her. When she even thought of his name she was tortured, mentally and physically, by a mixture of pain and desire that brought her close to desperation.

She wanted him, with deep emotional and sensual passion. She was burning alive. And when she thought that she would never fulfill this yearning it was like being under torture. When she forced herself to remember the moment that he had whispered Zara's name, she was torn on a rack of fire and electricity.

She finished her work and wandered through the rooms, looking out at the storm. Now that she had nothing to do, the fury in her heart was no longer kept at bay. It began to swamp her.

She wanted him, passionately, desperately. What difference did it make if he preferred her sister? What did it matter, in the scheme of things? *Jalal* was not to blame for the horrific experience of her past. It wasn't his fault if she had an unconscious inferiority complex that was looking to be reinforced....

She wanted him. She hadn't wanted a man for years, and now she wanted Jalal like someone who'd been starving in a desert and come on a feast of champagne and lobster served on gold plate.

He was a mirage. She knew that. He wasn't a man who would love her for her own sake. No good could come of it. Nothing would come of this...except sexual pleasure.

She was as sure of getting that as if she had a written guarantee.

For the first time since the age of sixteen she had a chance to experience true sexual passion. What if it was also the last time? What if she was destined never to feel such powerful desire for anyone again? What if she slipped back into that grey, featureless, sexless inner self again when he was gone?

The cat must come to me....

The storm increased in fury all around the little cottage, but it was no worse than the storm in Clio's heart.

Fourteen

She stood gazing blindly out the broad window at the crashing storm, drowning in whirlpools of thought. Then, against the cloudy darkness behind the glass, she saw a sudden flicker of light.

She whirled to stare at the lamp behind her, on the little table. The one she had tried to put on a while ago. Clio gazed at it, almost hypnotized, as it flickered twice more and then settled to its normal steady glow.

The generator was fixed, then.

He would be coming in.

She was raging with anguish, indecision and desire. She couldn't face Jalal, not feeling the way she was at this moment. She couldn't be locked up with him here, miles from nowhere, in a storm!

Oh, if only she had understood what she was thinking before! She had believed it was cut-and-dried, that she had all the strength necessary to resist her feelings for him.

If she had had any inkling, she would never have risked coming out with him today, not for anything! Too late she realized she should have told her mother, should have confided the whole story, rather than be forced into this situation.

She whirled and rushed into the kitchen, turning on lights as she went, filled the kettle and plugged it in. She was busily setting out cups and the jar of instant coffee and powdered creamer when he opened the kitchen door and stepped inside.

There was a simultaneous flash of lightning and deep roll of thunder. As if he were produced by the storm. A storm devil…

She lifted her head as he closed the door, and they stood for an immeasurable moment, staring at each other while the thunder rolled away into silence.

Then he said, "I have never seen so much rain in all my life as comes down in this country in five minutes."

It broke the mood, and Clio jerked into action. He was soaked to the skin, absolutely dripping.

"Stay right there!" she cried. "Don't move or you'll drip water everywhere!"

She opened the bag of dirty linen and dragged out a towel at random, tossing it on the floor at his feet. "Stand on that while I get you a fresh towel!"

She ran into the bathroom and dragged one of the towels from the stack of fresh ones she had placed there. When she returned to the kitchen, Jalal had stripped off his jacket.

"What will you do for clean towels, if I use that?" he asked, hesitating, as she offered him the towel across the kitchen counter.

"We can give them fresh ones at the house when they pick up the keys," she said with a shrug.

But he shook his head. "It isn't necessary. This will serve."

He was rubbing his hair with a dry corner of his jacket. His polo shirt was also well soaked over the shoulders and chest.

"You'd better take that off, and I'll throw it in the dryer," she said.

He threw her a look. "I am fine."

"Jalal, you're soaked!" It was her mother's voice in her. "You'll catch your death if you wander around like that!"

He smiled. "My death is not so easily caught as that."

"I mean, you'll get a cold."

"No," he said quietly. She gazed at him, half hypnotized, and got the message. She swallowed with difficulty.

The cat must come to me....

The kettle began to hiss, and she used the sound as an excuse to turn away and fuss with the tray.

Thunder rumbled overhead, then there was another huge, bright flash of lightning and a crack of thunder like a bomb exploding over the roof.

"Well, we won't be getting out of here for a while!" she said with false brightness, as if it hardly mattered.

He stiffened. "We can drive the boat in the rain, can't we?" Spying a row of hooks by the door, he flung his jacket onto one. "I have done it with your father."

"Not when it's as heavy as this, and not when there's lightning. Visibility's nil out on the lake in a deluge like this, and a boat on the water attracts lightning."

His jaw tightened as if that was the last thing he wanted

to hear, but he made no comment beyond a murmured "I see."

She had chills racing up and down her back, along her arms and legs. Was he thinking about how easy sex would be right now? She was. So easy. A moment out of time. Madness that would be a thing apart. She was melting with her own heat.

She swallowed and lifted the boiling kettle to pour water on the coffee in the carafe. The aroma caught her nostrils with another temptation of the senses, teasing her with one sensual stimulus into thinking of others....

She picked up the tray and moved into the sitting room, and after a pause while he kicked off his muddy deck shoes, Jalal followed. Thunder and lightning were now almost continuous in the heavens, and the sitting-room windows gave them a front-row seat on the magnificent drama.

It was a real downpour, coming in sheets. It thundered on the roof, made the water in the river leap and dance, turned paths into channels of mud.

Jalal sat in an armchair, nodding when she had poured his coffee, and picking it up off the tray she had set on the table before the sofa.

"Is so much rain usual? Is this why people come here?"

She smiled. "They usually come for the sun. But it's been a wet season so far. A storm like this happens every five years or so, I guess."

There was a fireplace. How pleasant it would be to light a fire, Clio dreamed, and sit here on the sofa with someone you loved...it really was a perfect cottage for honeymooners.

The main front windows looked out on the river, but the window also turned the corner of the house, so that a narrow strip, beside the fireplace, looked out over the forest. In the dangerous silence that fell between them, Clio sipped her coffee and nervously turned her head to watch the rain bucketing down on the trees....

"My God, the *cat!*" she cried. On automatic reflex she slapped her cup down on the table and jumped to her feet, staring.

Out there, just on this side of the bridge over the part of the river that ran behind the house, sat a half-drowned black-and-white cat, its pink mouth piteously open in a cry that was drowned by the storm.

"Wousky!" She cried its name, though of course the cat couldn't hear her. "Wousky!"

She rushed to the front door and tore it open, while behind her Jalal was getting to his feet. "Are you going to—" he began, but Clio was already out in the deluge.

Good grief, it was even worse than it looked! This was like standing under Niagara Falls! She was drenched to the skin in a second, her shoes turned to pails of water. She put up her hands to protect her eyes and stared at where she had last seen the cat.

It had crossed the damn bridge, she saw, and was sitting under a leafy plant, soaked and bedraggled to the last degree. Muttering curses, Clio splashed across the grassy clearing, over the picturesque little footbridge, calling its name.

"Wousky, Wousky! Kitty, kitty, kitty!"

The cat sat as if waiting for her, but as she got closer, suddenly got to its feet and shot away again.

She answers to her name, Clio remembered the Williamses assuring her. Dammit, why did no cat on earth ever answer to its name, and why did owners persist in imagining that they did?

"No!" Clio wailed, and her foot slipped and she fell

headlong, landing full length in thick sloppy mud. "Oh, damn you, Wousky!" she cried. She struggled to her feet, covered in mud, just as Jalal arrived beside her.

Lightning illuminated the scene, and there the cat was, a few yards away, its pink mouth open, repeating the cry. Directly overhead the thunder cracked and rattled and applauded as if this were all a game.

"Wousky!" She tried again, taking another few steps. The cat waited as if wanting to be caught; then again, as she got close, dashed away.

"What are you doing? The cat will not let you catch her!" Jalal shouted.

"Yes," she contradicted him, pushing her mud-caked hair out of her face. "She's trying to tell us something. She's trying to lead us somewhere. Okay, Wousky, what is it?"

It wasn't unknown for an animal to lead humans to other humans or animals in trouble, and her heart was now kicking uncomfortably.

Wousky led them on into the forest, turning every few feet to check that they were following. Under the thick cover of the forest at least the rain was not so drowningly heavy, but wet leaves slapped them unmercifully, and Clio was starting to shiver.

"Can we find our way back?" Jalal asked.

Clio turned to glance back. Through the trees there was a tiny glow of light. "If she doesn't take us too much further we'll be okay."

Just then the cat stopped, beside a tree, wailing now in a voice that could be heard. "What *is* it?" Clio wondered, drawing close.

Then she saw. "Oh, my! Oh, *Wousky!*" she crooned.

In a hollow under a raised root, the cat had formed a nest. It must have seemed perfect when she built it, but the rain had turned it into a mudhole. She had done her best, dragging her tiny kittens up the slope of the hollow, but it had clearly filled deeper and deeper with water, and the kittens were now so far out they were exposed to the rain.

"Oh, Wousky, what a clever cat you are!" Clio told the anxious mother. She smiled at Jalal, who had squatted beside her. "Isn't that amazing? She must have realized we were there when the lights went on and come to get us!"

"This one is half drowned already," Jalal said, reaching carefully to pick up a kitten lying half in the puddle.

The mother moved anxiously to his side, watching as he examined the muddy kitten on his strong, safe palm. He stroked it with one finger, until he was rewarded with a pink-mouthed complaint.

Clio laughed in delighted relief. "Okay, we're going to fix this little problem, Wousky, don't you worry!" she cried.

One by one, she began to pick up the tiny bedraggled lumps of fur and, lifting her mud-stained T-shirt at the waist, she laid them carefully inside the little hammock that was formed.

"Four altogether," she said. "Is that all of them?"

Jalal was still carrying the one he had rescued. He bent over and ran his free hand through the puddle, dredging for bodies, then looked all around the area.

"I think we have them all," he said.

The cat made no complaint as they got to their feet and turned to leave, so they searched no further. With half-agitated, half-approving cries, Wousky rushed along the path and back to them, as if urging them to hurry.

They followed the light through the trees and came out at the bridge again. The rain was still torrential. In a few more minutes they were stepping inside the kitchen door. After such drama, it was almost strange to feel the peace of the cottage enclose them again.

Clio rinsed the mud from the kittens under the warm tap, making sure noses and mouths were clean and in working order, and then made a nest of some of last week's used towels beside the fireplace, where Wousky, after scoffing a huge amount of dinner, immediately settled down with the kittens and started to purr and lick.

Jalal meanwhile had lit a fire. Clio plugged in the space heater and drew it to the other side of the kittens' nest to give them more immediate warmth.

Then she got to her feet and stood looking down at herself. She was mud from head to foot. Jalal was almost as bad.

"Okay, I think we're next," she said.

Clio emerged from the shower wrapped in a huge towel, another one wrapping her hair. Jalal was where she had left him, in the kitchen, leaning against the counter, his arms across his chest, coffee cup in his hand.

She couldn't look directly at him as she moved past him to the washing machine.

"Your turn," she said, busily stuffing her muddy garments into it. "If you toss your things out, I'll put everything in the washer together."

Behind her she heard him set down his cup and move towards the bathroom. When the door closed, she heaved a massive sigh, trying to let go of the tension that gripped her.

A moment later, he did as she suggested, tossing his clothes out the bathroom door. Clio bent to pick them up, and heard the shower start again, and suddenly her mind was a jumble of erotic images of Jalal naked.

She gasped, leaning against the wall, while a sensual flood assailed her body and mind. She thought of the water hitting his body, saw the curling black hair on his chest, his hand stroking soap into it, the water drumming it into bubbles, the suds caressing his muscles, rinsing down his chest, his arms, his thighs, knees, ankles…those strong bare feet.

She heard the soft sound of him blowing water out, and knew that he was standing with his head under the stream, saw the water in his dark eyelashes, squeezed shut, on his lips….

The sound of the shower stopped suddenly, and she leapt guiltily, as though he might open the door the next second and catch her there, melting with passion for him.

She grabbed up his things and moved over to the washer, and, stuffing them in, added detergent and turned the dial. Water gushed into the machine and she held it, feeling the vibration under her hands.

She needed strength. She needed to think. But she was incapable of thinking, with him naked in the next room….

She could hear him moving around, and thought, *No wonder this place is popular with honeymooners!* The air seemed to have an erotic charge, as if the memory of passion had soaked into the fabric of the place, steeping the beams themselves with sensuality.

She fled into the sitting room, where Wousky, half-asleep, was purring in her nest, all her little ones glued to her teats, throbbing with the sensual pleasure of warm milk and the closeness of their mother's body.

Outside the rain still hammered down.

Clio went back to the kitchen and called up the main house on the CB radio. Her mother answered.

"Everything has ground to a halt here," Maddy said, after a few moments' chat. "We're just waiting for it to stop. I imagine people have stopped on the road to do the same. Stupid to try to drive in rain like this.''

''We'll be back when it's over,'' Clio said, and a moment later they signed off.

The thunder and lightning had passed over, and now it had settled down to a steady downpour. Clio stood in the sitting room staring out. She could see her own reflection in the glass, superimposed on the river and the rain.

She saw Jalal, a huge towel wrapped around his waist, a smaller one slung over his shoulders and naked chest, enter the room behind her.

Fifteen

She stayed where she was, staring into the glass, watching as he stepped slowly across the room towards her. When he was still several feet away she could feel his presence against her skin. Her body, already pumping with heat, leapt into sensual awareness as if his hand stroked her.

He stopped close behind her, and she saw how his head tilted as he looked down at her. Still she could not look at him directly.

Slowly his hand came up and cupped her naked shoulder. She twitched with the electricity that jolted through her, and swallowed, her lips pressed tight.

"Clio," he said softly. His other hand came up, and he gently, inexorably, turned her to face him.

"Look at me."

Her heart was leaping all over her body with fear, nerves, need. She raised her eyes and felt another powerful connection as their gaze met.

"Are you afraid?"

She looked away and gasped for air, sighing it tremblingly out. "A little, I guess," she admitted.

"Do not be afraid. We will go no further than you wish, now or any time. There will not come a point when I push you beyond what you can accept."

She was silent, staring out at the storm. The contented sound of the mother cat singing the song of security to her kittens purred on the air.

"Can you trust me to keep my word in this?"

"Look…" She licked her lips. "I'll be all right, it's just—if you could just…not say her name. I know you—"

Jalal moved one hand to lift her chin, making her eyes meet his. He was frowning. "What does this mean? 'Not say her name'?"

"A long time ago there was a guy who loved Zara and took me as second best, and it was—I was young, Jalal, it wasn't a good experience, it kind of—left me…raw." Her voice was trembling, though she was fighting to speak calmly. She swallowed against the huge lump of feeling in her throat and wondered if she could go any further with this.

He was listening closely. "He forced you against your will, wanting your sister?" he asked gently, masking his outrage.

"No…" she sighed on a sad, long outbreath. "No, he didn't force anything. It was just that…I didn't know till it was too late—almost too late—" she corrected herself ruthlessly "—that he was pretending I was Zara." She looked up at him, trying to smile matter-of-factly. "He said her name, and then I knew."

He was silent for long moments, so still as he watched

her that she imagined he understood and she wouldn't have to explain further.

"And what do you fear now? Are you afraid that I, too, will say the name of some other woman? I will speak no name but yours. I think no name but yours, Clio," he whispered urgently.

Desire and anguish in equal measure clutched at her.

"It's just—when you said her name last time, it just cut through me, I'm sorry. And if you did it ag—"

She realized, with a suddenly sinking heart, that she could not go through with it. She could not do this, no matter how desperately she wanted him. She couldn't do it to herself, knowingly make love with a man who loved someone else, fearing all the time that he might whisper her name.

"Whose name?" he demanded, frowning.

"I'm sorry," she said after a moment. "I can't do this after all."

"I said no one's name."

If he didn't even remember the moment, how could she hope that he would be able to control the impulse?

"Jalal, it doesn't really matter—"

"If you think I spoke another woman's name while making love to you, it matters very much! Whose name do you believe you heard me say?"

His certainty was so convincing. But she *had* heard it—she hadn't imagined it.

"Zara's. Maybe you didn't realize—"

"*Zara's!*" He was completely surprised, incredulous. "Why should I say your sister's name in such a moment? It is ridiculous! Do you believe that I desire my uncle's wife? I do not. What could you have heard? What did you imagine?"

She stared at the strong pulse in the top of his throat, the thick red terry cloth of the towel around his neck.

She took a deep breath, the better to stand her ground. "I didn't imagine it. I heard it. You said, *Zary*. As plain as day." She cleared her throat. "Funny, Zary is what I called her when we were kids. I didn't think anyone else ever used it."

"Zarie," he repeated, testing the word. He began to shake his head, but stopped. His eyes narrowed with concentration.

"*Zahri*," he said, in another voice, as light dawned. "I called you *zahri*, is this what you heard?"

"Yes!" she said, suddenly hearing it again, the little explosion of breath on the vowel. "Yes, that was it! You said it."

"I said it, yes." He nodded. "This word means *my flower* in Arabic." His hand encircled her throat and gently tilted her chin. "I was not speaking of your sister, but of you. Of the flower of your beautiful body, that I wanted so much to open for me."

A storm of sensation coursed through her, blowing her flat. Clio's head fell back. She sighed out all her pent-up tension and anguish on a long moan of surrender.

"And this is all there is to fear?" he demanded in a harsh whisper. "There is no other torment in your past—only this one word?"

She took a deep breath, trying to cope with the sensations that were rushing up and down and over her skin in a thousand directions at once. Suddenly she felt she wanted to weep.

She sniffed, and a breath of air escaped from her throat on a half sob. "That's it!" she said brightly. "That's all she wrote!"

Without another word Jalal bent and slipped an arm

under her knees and, lifting her high in his strong arms, turned towards the bedroom.

Beside the bed he set her on her feet, and as he did so the towel around her body began to slip from its moorings. She clutched at it, but he caught her wrist.

"Let me see you," he ordered.

At the tone of sheer possessiveness in his voice, she melted into fainting stillness. He clasped her other wrist and held both hands helplessly away from her body, his eyes burning into her as the towel slipped and spiralled around her breasts and hips like a lover's hands, and fell to the floor.

He stood gazing at her.

Intensely dark brown eyes under strong brows such as the poets loved, questioning, nervous, and watching him with such a strength of wanting his heart kicked brutally with answering hunger. Her wide, mobile lips alternately smiling and pressing against each other, wet and shining where she licked them, a pink that matched the dark pink nipples shivering to awareness under his gaze as it travelled down to those high, heavy breasts. A long, slender waist curving into sloping hips that invited a hand's caress...long smooth legs...

"You are a beautiful woman," he breathed hoarsely. "Poems have been written about you for a thousand years, and I did not know."

"About me?" She smiled.

He nodded. "They called you *Asheeq.*"

Her wide mouth moved, tremulous with feeling. "What does it mean?"

"Beloved," he murmured. "*Asheeq* is Beloved. *Anti asheeqi.*"

He lifted his other hand to the bright towel that wrapped

her hair, and pulled it free. Her wet hair fell heavily over one shoulder and down her back. She shivered as its weight pulled her scalp, caressed her skin. She trembled at the look in his eyes.

Passionate desire such as she had never experienced flowered and blossomed in her in bright bursts, as if a rich, thick garden burst into ripe fullness in the space of seconds. Perfume, colour, the silky touch of new petals crowded her senses all at once, stroking her into wild anticipation....

And he had scarcely touched her save with his eyes. Clio was almost frightened for what would happen when he touched her with his hands.

Slowly, still watching her, he pulled the towel from around his own neck and dropped it to the floor. Then his hands carefully, irresistibly, cupped her shoulders, drew her against his body, made her breasts press his warm naked chest, her thighs brush the thick terry that covered his muscled thighs. His head bent and his mouth tasted hers...and then devoured it with a suddenness that made her gasp.

His hunger for her melted her into wildest need. When his hand clasped her head to pull her lips more urgently against his, when his arm encircled her back to drag her tight against him, her body sensed his deep hunger and sent thrilling heat through her. When his fingers squeezed and his palms pressed her back, thighs, arms, urgent messages zipped along her nerves, igniting fire beacons everywhere to signal her hunger to her whole body.

After an eternity of kisses, gentle and passionate, teasing, tasting, urgent...his lips left hers.

"Lie down," he said.

She turned in his hold to the high mattress and drew off the spread, tossing it down to the foot, hiked one knee up, then the other, and slipped on all fours towards the centre of the wide bed.

She heard a gasp of indrawn breath, and his hands enclosed her hips in firm command, stopping her where she was.

And then, before she knew what was happening, his mouth came at her from behind, directed with unerring suddenness between her legs, its damp heat thrusting sharp pleasure against the nerve centre of her being.

She cried out uncontrollably. And again. She tried to move, for the pleasure was unfamiliarly shocking her system, but his hands grasped her thighs, irresistibly, pulling them apart to give him better access. She was pinned to the place, by his grip and by the pleasure that poured through her, raising her desire to a pitch she hadn't known existed.

She could do nothing except wait, her thighs opening uncontrollably to his mouth, her knees spreading further, her whole body listening to the buildup of nearly intolerable sweet need as his tongue stroked, rasped, caressed, pushed the pleasured anticipation along her nerves.

She had expected nothing like this. So quick, so overwhelming, a need so desperate it was almost rage. She began to whimper her urgent need for release from his tongue's hungry stroking, his mouth's hot embrace, from the savage yearning they made her feel.

He went on with that wild, rough, relentless caress, building the torment till it could hardly be borne. Her mind reeled and she lost herself—to a primitive, barbarian, all-consuming need that she had hidden from herself for too long.

She pressed her upper body down, clutching a pillow and burying her face in it, moaning, arching her body to his mouth without shame—totally, utterly dedicated to her own pleasure.

Then at last it happened: hot, sweet release began a slow spiral out from under his mouth and poured over all her skin and muscles, to every fingernail, to each single hair tip. As the throbbing pleasure reached her throat Clio cried aloud, a long, haunting cry of gratitude and release.

When it had passed, she collapsed flat on the bed, and six and a half years of pent-up need flowed and flowered and was satisfied in her.

"Oh, thank you! Oh, Jalal, that was so sweet!" she murmured to the pillow in a husky, sensual voice that made his eyes narrow as he looked at her. "Oh, so delicious! Oh, was there ever anything like that since the dawn of history! Will there ever be anything like it again!"

Behind her, dropping his own towel to the floor, he smiled.

"I think I can promise that there will be," Jalal said softly.

Languidly she rolled over and lay with her head curved at an angle to look at him. His body was so beautiful. As he stretched out on the bed beside her, she admired the flexing and contracting of his whole musculature, the gorgeous shape of him, the hard, hungry, long, strong sex.

She looked away to catch her breath, and he came down beside her, one hand carefully enclosing her breast, the other tangling in her damp hair.

She stroked his cheek, smiling lazily, brushed the generous lips. He drew her finger into his mouth and sucked it, and as pleasure contracted in her abdomen the spiral of tension started again. She grunted softly.

His hand strayed again to the mat of pleasure-dampened hair between her thighs, and his thumb toyed there, watching while her eyelids fluttered. Her hands sought out his body, and stroked him, feeling with delighted curiosity where he was smooth and where hair roughened his skin, how muscle curved into muscle....

When she touched his engorged sex his eyes narrowed and his lips parted in a deeply erotic smile, his teeth flashing white. She explored the smooth hardness with a joy she could hardly contain, swept with a wanton, hungry flood of feeling she had believed herself incapable of.

"Oh, I love this!" she cried, her hand tightening possessively on him.

Then, as his hand stroked her to a sudden second release, she arched her back, thrusting her hips up, and as the pleasure peaked and sank away he was suddenly above her, moving his legs between hers as she willingly opened herself to him.

Her pleasure had barely ebbed when he pushed into the hot pulsing rose. It enclosed him with hungry gratitude, and he thrust further and further in, till he had reached his length in her. He heard her cry of satisfaction then, and knew he had waited all his life for such a cry.

He wrested himself from the rose's loving embrace, and wildly thrust home again, and she grunted with such deep surprise he gasped in a fierce, almost uncontrolled response.

He pounded into her over and over, each thrust causing a savage pulse of pleasure through her system. Helplessly she cried his name, and then she wordlessly moaned, and then, losing her knowledge of time, of place, of self, she sank into a wordless thirst for the pleasure he gave her, drinking it in with choking, desperate sighs.

Only pleasure mattered now, pleasure that shimmered out beyond her own body, so that she felt her joy as far as she could reach, and in the air that surrounded them.

With crazy, unbelieving joy she stroked the marvellous body, felt how the strong back, the clenching buttocks, the powerful shoulders and thighs moved under her hands, felt how the hard masculine sex moved within her.

He bent his head, murmuring, and smothered her mouth with a hungry kiss, thrusting as wildly with his tongue as with his body, to drive them both beyond the reach of everything they knew, deep into the unknown.

She heard his wild cry and felt the pulsing throb of his sex in her, in the same moment, and at last more pleasure than her system could hold burst through her. She arched up to meet his body's desperate thrust, and again, and again, and then wild pleasure coursed through them, seeking and finding that timeless place they sought, in the Other.

Sixteen

They lay in each other's embrace, listening to their heart-beats reflected in the rain. His arm was around her, Clio's head nesting in the curve of his shoulder, her arm lying across his chest, her hand lazily stroking his shoulder and arm.

She was humming a tuneless hum, just on the breath, without knowing it. He lay listening, a smile pulling at his lips.

"You are like the cat," Jalal murmured.

"Mmm? I am?"

"You are purring."

Suddenly hearing her own song for the first time, she laughed. "I suppose I am."

"Do you always purr at such moments?" he asked. It was a jealous question. He would not have voiced it if he had known what he was going to say.

"I've never had such a moment before, so I wouldn't know," Clio replied in a matter-of-fact tone.

His fingers, stroking her flank lazily, stilled.

"Never had—what do you mean? Do you tell me that no man has before known how to please a woman of such passion as you? What sort of men does this culture produce?"

"Oh, plenty of dedicated ones, really." She lifted herself on an elbow and smiled down at him. "I've been in a cage. Some very nice guys tried, but no one before you could find the key."

It shook Jalal to the core. He kissed her with an abrupt surge of passion, rolled her over on her back, and thrust his way inside again. She gasped and melted with the suddenness of it, and, her body still swollen with fulfilled desire, accepted his wild thrusting with mews of delight. Almost at once she was driven up to the peak again, and over, crying wildly, feeling how his hands, wrapped in her hair and around her wrist, clenched with his own joy.

"Mmm," she sighed appreciatively, when they had become calm again, and he found that that sound in her throat stirred him to his core. It was necessary to him now, like water, and he suddenly felt it would be so forever. He had been seeking something all his life, but had only known that it was so when he found what he sought.

Jalal kissed her lightly on her sweat-damp shoulder, loving her passionate openness and responsiveness. That such a woman had found so little joy in a body made for pleasure was almost unbelievable.

"You have—what do you say?—some catching up to do."

"Years," she agreed with a smile at once satisfied and longing.

"Perhaps it can be condensed."

She glinted at him with a glance of such sensually charged abandon that he felt it like a blow.

But as he reached for her again she sat up, her damp hair tousled all around her shoulders, smiling down at him with lazy, pleasure-sated eyes.

"I wish we could stay here all night," she said. "But people will be arriving as soon as the rain lets up."

She slipped off the bed and padded into the kitchen, where she quickly transferred their clothes from washer to dryer. She returned to the bedroom and bent to pick up the scattered towels, then hesitated. He was just getting to his feet.

"Do you want another shower?"

He looked at her, sex on his mind. "Yes," he said. "Let us go to the shower."

She melted where she stood, dropping the towels again, and let him lead her into the bathroom. The stone-tiled floor was cool underfoot, adding another sensual input to her already overloaded nerve pathways. When the soft flow of water came down over them, she sighed with delight.

He caught her under the buttocks. "Put your legs around me," he muttered, and she could only moan in anticipation and obey, wrapping herself around his hips, opening her thighs to the magnificent body, ready for her again.

He set her back against the shower wall, grasped her thighs, and slipped hungrily between the soft petals of the rose again.

Water and pleasure simultaneously flowed over and through their bodies, soft and delicious, combining into a sweet rosewater that their senses could taste. He thrust a little, then paused and, supporting her with one hand, lifted the other to the bud of the rose, and caressed it till her tears of joy mingled with the water that poured so luxuriously over them, and her clenching, spasmodic submission to the pleasure brought him his own release.

The rain abated. They tidied the cottage, laundered the sheets and remade the bed, leaving the towels they had used still whirling in the dryer, and a note on the table for the renters. Then they carefully set the kittens into a small cardboard box and Jalal carried it down to the boat, with Wousky anxiously watching from a supervisory position over Clio's shoulder.

The sky was clearing, the sun breaking through to make an appearance over a wet world. She stood within the circle of his arm as he steered the boat for home, and felt a closeness she hadn't felt for a man since that night with Peter, and a lightness of spirit she had hardly imagined possible.

"I want to know about this man who hurt you," he said. "Will you tell me the story?"

"I've never told anyone," Clio murmured, half to herself. No wonder the incident had had such a hold over her imagination. She had never known how to tell even her mother about such deep humiliation, and of course she had never told Zara, but she could tell Jalal.

"He was kind of what you'd call my high school crush," she began. "I was thirteen and just starting, and he was in his final year. I thought he was so gorgeous...."

She took him through it, step by step, and as they sped across the lake, the clouds dispersed completely and the sun glowed over the scene, all so clean and fresh after such thorough washing, and it really seemed like a metaphor for her own soul. All the anguish, all the dust of the past, washed away by Jalal's passion.

His face hardened when she described that night when

she had lost so much more than her innocence, but he didn't interrupt.

"What does that mean, jailbait?" he asked when she had arrived at the bitter end.

"For a guy of nineteen or twenty to make love with a girl under sixteen is illegal here, even if she consents," she explained. "He could have gone to prison if he hadn't waited till I was at the legal age of consent."

He was silent as they headed under a picturesque bridge. "Oh, someone's in the MacAllister place," Clio observed absently when they came out the other side.

Jalal looked startled. "Pardon?"

She pointed through the plastic window of the rain hood. "See them up there on the deck?"

He glanced up as they passed the mansion-sized summer house, but didn't answer.

"What has happened to Peter?" he went on after a moment.

"Happened?"

"Has he married?"

"Married? Golly, no, he's only twenty-five or six! He still runs his father's car dealership, last time I looked. I guess he dates, but I have no idea who. I saw him once in the street a couple of years ago. He was driving yet another splashy sports car. I don't suppose he'll want to trade that in for a station wagon for a long time yet."

"He is a fool," Jalal said with an amused smile, as if Peter were about as important as last week's newspaper.

Clio laughed, light and free. "The sun's out, let's take the rain hood down!" she said, and he stopped the boat and they quickly did so.

"Now," he said, as if he understood more than she had

said. "Now the wind will blow tangles into your hair. And tonight...tonight I want to lie in the tangles again."

"Of course he is interested," Saifuddin ar Ratib said carefully. "He would not wish to commit himself until he sees exactly what we have to offer."

"He must be made to commit himself," said the voice at the other end of the phone.

"Of course, Excellency."

"If I made myself known to him too soon, he might be tempted to expose me to his uncles in exchange for a return to their good favour. We must have him compromised first."

"Can he possibly have any loyalty to them? Do you fear it? A man who has been sent into exile?"

"Did you not tell me you sensed that he had some sentimental attachment to them?"

"I did, Excellency. Partly perhaps because he feels he owes the course of his life, his education, to the care of his grandfather the king."

At the other end of the wire there was a thoughtful pause. "You are right, as always, Saifuddin. Now is the time to tell him. Call me again when it is done."

Jalal was late for dinner. He had taken a boat out, no one knew where, shortly after he and Clio brought the cat and kittens back from Solitaire. It wasn't usual for Jalal to miss a family meal without warning, and everybody was wondering what had happened.

Clio's worries now had more, not less potency. What if she had to choose between loyalties? If Jalal was conspiring against the princes—

It was the evening of their regular self-defence class, which made the children even more anxious. "He always says discipline is important, so he wouldn't just miss the class,'' Ben said.

''Well, then, he'll be back in time for the class,'' Maddy said. ''Will you all please stop worrying? Some-one phoned for Jalal and I gave him the message when he got in. He probably went to see someone and just got delayed.''

Did he have an accent? The question arose in her mind completely against her will, but Clio gritted her teeth and managed not to speak it aloud.

''Where *is* Jalal?'' Donnelly asked in a hopeless voice, for the third time, and Clio smiled at her with deep fellow feeling. Donnelly was right—the family group was not complete without him.

The sound of a boat engine made them all stop talking to listen. It came closer, making all the familiar noises of drawing up at the family dock, and the kids began to smile and sigh with relief.

Clio bit her tongue to stop herself smiling too much, but when Jalal's light footstep was heard on the verandah and he came through the door, she was grinning as broadly even as Donnelly.

''Jalal, Jalal!'' the child cried in her sweet, piercing voice, as if the end of the world had been averted at the last minute.

He came in smiling, picked up his plate from the table in a way that had become totally familiar, and went to the stove to pluck a cob of corn from the pot there.

Everyone was chatting, relaxed, happy. Jalal sat down at the table and flicked Clio a glance so loaded her heart started jumping like a sheep caught in a fence. Her father said something, her mother replied, and the river of life flowed on in the big friendly kitchen as it had always done.

Clio marvelled that she could sit in the middle of all the usual family row, and connect to Jalal as intimately as if they were alone on an island...and know that, in the last couple of hours, wherever he had gone, something had happened to worry him.

When supper was over and the dishwasher stacked, it was time for the self-defence class. Surrounded by kids, Jalal flicked Clio a glance. She nodded with her eyelashes, swallowed convulsively, and felt her cheeks go hot. When she risked another look at him his jaw was tight with brutally imposed self-control.

They all rushed out, leaving Clio with her parents in the kitchen. A part of her had wanted him to cancel the class, but she knew he couldn't. You couldn't teach self-discipline without practising it.

So she helped her mother as usual in the kitchen, and then, turning down a TV film, went upstairs, to while away the time in luscious anticipation and sybaritic preparation till he could come to her.

She bathed in her sexiest perfumed bath oil, an expensive Christmas present she had never used before, and conditioned her hair, and gave herself a manicure and a pedicure, painting her nails a creamy bronze that matched her tan. She rubbed body satin everywhere.

She sprayed perfume into her hair, blew it dry and left it to spread freely over her shoulders and back.

But when it came time to dress, she discovered a gap in her wardrobe that she had never noticed before: she did not have one lacy, sexy nightgown or piece of underwear anywhere in her drawers. There was the little turquoise silk slip and matching robe her parents had given her for her last birthday, and that was the closest thing she had to a garment deliberately designed to ignite a man's desire.

In the end, she slipped on one of Jude's cast-off shirts in peach oxford cotton. It was worn and a little frayed, but blissfully soft.

And underneath…only her own brown body, already melting at the thought that he would soon be here, leaping with excitement when, a few moments later, she heard the soft footfall on the stairs, igniting into ready flame when the tap on the door was followed by her dark lover….

Clio was lying on one elbow on the bed, with a book that she hadn't been able to read a word of, the room softly lighted, the window of her tiny balcony open on a magical night. Soft blues wafted from the speakers of her CD player. Outside the lake glinted with the reflected light of moon and stars and the lamps of the houses around its shores. A fresh breeze stirred the open curtains, caught his robe as he turned to shut the bedroom door behind him.

He stood for a moment looking down at her. Jalal dressed like a Westerner during the day, but at night, when relaxing, he sometimes reverted to the clothes of his homeland. Tonight he was wearing an oriental-print green-and-gold dressing gown in flowing cotton, open over a bare chest and loose trousers tied at the waist. He looked like a fantasy sheikh.

The sight of him, so dark and exotic in the strong colours, made her heart beat even faster. She tilted her chin to smile at him, and he bent over her and kissed her.

She lifted her arms around his neck as he sank down on the bed over her. She felt his hands busy with the buttons on her shirt, and then he pushed the soft fabric aside and he lifted his head and his eyes and his hand stroked her bare shoulder, her breast, her stomach. Then he drew her naked breasts against his warm chest and devoured her lips with another kiss.

She was already on fire with need, with the memory of the pleasure he could give her, with deep anticipation. She moaned against his mouth and felt his body leap in response.

"I hunger for you, Clio," he murmured against her lips, with a fierce desperation that thrilled her with longing. "Kiss me, kiss me."

Shivers of electric feeling burnt over her body, making her womb melt into readiness, lifting her rosebud nipples to his attention. She felt with hungry, yearning abruptness that she could never get enough of him, that until their bodies and souls fused forever into one being she would not have what she sought from him.

He rolled over onto his back, drawing her onto his chest, cupping her head and kissing her again. She lifted her head and gazed down into his eyes with hungry urgency.

"I love you," she whispered, and gasped as she heard her own words, understanding their truth only as she heard them.

"I love you, Clio," Jalal said, and her heart beat with such crazy wildness she couldn't find breath.

Seventeen

His two hands came up to encircle her head as if she were both precious and fragile, a perfect rose, and his dark eyes gazed into hers.

"You looked at me at the wedding, do you remember? And you said, *We will never be friends*...."

"I remember," she murmured, ashamed.

"I knew then. I knew that you were right—not friends, we were not destined to be friends, you and I, but much more. I knew then that I would not rest until you called me Lover."

She smiled, though tears were burning her eyes. "Lover," she whispered.

His mouth trailed sweet fire along the underside of her chin, her ear, and down her throat to the pulse that beat there.

"*Asheeqi*," he murmured there, and monitored with his lips the pulse's leap into wild disarray.

Under her shirt his hands caressed her back, her waist, her thighs, with a firm, hungry possessiveness that thrilled and burned her. His eyes were like doorways into the black depths of the universe, and he gazed at her, drinking her in.

His fingers slipped between her thighs and began to toy with the rose with a touch like the brush of silk. He smiled and watched her response, watched her eyes lose focus, her eyelids droop, her mouth purse and swell with sensuous swooning.

When her hips began to press against him, he rolled her over onto her back and lay above her, one arm under her head, his other hand trailing in the mat of hair that hid the petals of the rose. He cupped one thigh and drew it aside, to give his hand and his eyes better access. And then his fingers began a sweet, slow torment of stroking amongst the damp petals, and around the pulsing bud, over and over and over, with the utmost patience.

Unbelievably delicious sensations began to uncurl in her at this urging, an intensely burning fire without flame followed the trail that his finger drew on her flesh, a heat that was almost unbearable, a sweetness sweeter than the sweetest sugar....

He was in no hurry. He did not try to rush her, though at any time he could have brought the pleasure on her just by applying a more concentrated pressure...he just went on, slowly and deliberately, drawing lines of fire over her skin that reached deep inside her body.

When the pleasure slowly spiralled out in her at last, needing no effort from her, nothing but to lie and accept it, it was so intense that she did not know whether it was pleasure or pain that she felt. All she knew was how her whole body drank it in, like a starved desert in a flood.

Only when it was over could she make a sound, so

intently had she been listening to the physical joy he gave
her. Then she gasped, and sighed, and told him her gratitude with words and smiles and wordless moans.

They kissed and toyed, and laughed with total joy. And
then Jalal stripped off his robe and his trousers and lay
down again beside her, and her breath hissed between her
teeth as she admired his handsome body, the instrument
of her pleasure.

"Come over me," he said. He suited the action to the
word by drawing her thigh over his, till she was above
him on her knees, her hair falling down her back, her
thighs parted over his.

He drew her hips down and fitted their bodies together,
and pulled her firmly down against him, and together they
grunted their satisfaction at this union.

He reached up to strip off the shirt that still swathed
her shoulders, dragged it down her arms, and tossed it
aside, and then his hands cupped and caressed her shoulders, ran along her upper arms, trailed across her midriff
and slipped up to curl over the full, heavy breasts.

At the same time he moved in her, hard, and she gasped
and fell forward onto her hands, so that her breasts were
pressed into his hold, and her hips began involuntarily
writhing against the pleasure of him inside her.

He thrust in her, watching how the concentration of
pleasure was mirrored in her face, and when her body
began to push and seek, he grasped her hips, pulling her
body against his, so that the joy fountained up and gave
her the release she sought.

She sank down against him, her breasts pressing his
chest, her mouth against his ear, sighing the little noises
of gratitude that made his flesh leap. He pulled her face
over his and kissed her, knowing that never before had he
taken such pleasure in the giving of pleasure. Feeling for

the first time that to give one woman pleasure could be enough for a man, all his life long.

She was moving against him in a search for more, and he gripped her thighs and moved her against him till her body's clenching response relaxed.

"Now," he murmured, and rolled over with her again, and this time he rose above her, their bodies still joined. His thighs pushed her thighs wide apart, and he began to thrust with hard, purposeful thrusts, deep within.

She grunted in hunger, and she knew that what he had given her had merely ignited her whole body, to prepare it for this. Each thrust was a whole new world of intense physical sensation, as if he reached inside her soul....

She tossed her head as her cries became wilder and wilder, and she lost her awareness of the room, the light— she was aware only of pleasure. Even self was gone, even Jalal was lost in the cloudy haze of physical and mental sensation, the deepest, maddest pleasure she could possibly imagine, and more.

Still he drove into her, on and on, until time also had no meaning, until for both of them there was only the depths of darkness, where the jewel they sought lay hidden, but sending out shafts of fire....

They entered the utter darkness, then, and clasped the jewel, and its light shimmered through their united selves until they cried out in helpless gratitude with the perfect joy, perfect knowledge the jewel contained, and its blinding light.

"What has worried you tonight?" she asked, lying with him in the still night, with music playing softly.

He was silent. Then, "It is nothing to do with anything here. Nothing to do with your fam—"

Then he remembered Zara, and broke off.

Her heart began to beat in hard, anxious thuds. "Is it something to do with Barakat?"

He sighed. "If I tell you, Clio, it will be to put a burden on you that you can share with no one. You can mention it to no other living soul. Do you wish for such a burden?"

"Oh, God," she whispered. "I'm not sure I can stand this. How—what kind of a burden?" If it was the burden of choosing between his happiness and Zara's...how could she bear it?

He wound a hand in her hair. "It would be very dangerous if you spoke of it. You must understand that lives will be in danger. Do you accept to know?"

"Is one of the lives yours?"

He was silent, merely gazing at her from his dark eyes, but she knew.

"Is—is one Zara's?"

Jalal took a breath and stroked her hair, down over her scalp and where it lay across her shoulder. "I am doing my best to see that this is not a danger."

"Oh, my God!" Clio closed her eyes painfully. "I don't think I want to know."

They were silent for a moment, while she wondered if she had made the coward's choice. Could he be the man he was, the man she knew him to be, and be plotting a horror? And yet—if he *was* conspiring with someone—shouldn't she try to find out?

But she was afraid to hear something that would destroy her newfound joy. One day? Was that all that was allotted to her? No, she couldn't face that. What would it hurt if she lived in ignorance a few more days?

"I may have to return soon to Barakat," Jalal said suddenly. His hand grasped hers, and he kissed it. "If I go, Clio—will you go with me?"

Her heart kicked painfully. The change was too quick for her. "What?"

"If circumstances call me home—come with me, Clio."

"To the Emirates?" she almost wailed. "For how long? It's right in the busiest part of the season!"

"For how long? Forever! Will you marry me? I love you, Clio. I want you to come home with me. Please be my wife."

She gazed into his face, her heart racing and kicking. Warmth seemed to pulse through her system, as if love had its own pathways that also came from the heart. But—

"Oh, Jalal."

"Say yes."

"Go away from here? Forever?"

He reached for her, and drew her into his arms. She clung to him. Her eyes moved around her room, pausing at the curtains billowing on the night breeze, and she listened to the magic cry of the lake.

Owl, and Bear, and Wolf seemed to cry out to her from the distant hills. She would not hear their voices anymore, in the desert.

"We will visit," he said.

"I can't!" she breathed. "Jalal, it's my home!"

"I will give you a new home. A palace, with fountains and beautiful things. We will not be far from the mountains...."

"I can't go and live in another country! I belong here!"

His eyes darkened. It was her early reaction. Women softened in such matters where they loved...if she loved. It was a woman's role to follow her husband.

Abruptly he thought of his grandmother, her broken-hearted yearning for the high country of her youth. If he took Clio back to Barakat, would she also tell her children stories of the land she loved and longed for? But if he did not, how would he survive?

"Clio, I have found you now. You are everything to me. Do not you love me?"

Tears burned her eyes. "I love you! I love you, I want to be with you! But—oh, Jalal, please don't ask me this!"

He had no answer. He drew her down and kissed her with urgent passion, covering her body with his own, seeking solace for his tormented soul within.

The morning was bright after the previous day's torrential rain; it was going to be a scorcher.

"You're going to be swamped in the ice cream shop today, and last night's delivery didn't get through," Maddy commented over breakfast.

Clio was grateful for the necessity to concentrate on everyday things. She had awakened depressed and didn't want to think about the choice facing her. Why was love so full of pain? It was supposed to be wonderful.

In the small hours of the morning, Jalal had left her, and she had fallen asleep before he returned. When she awoke this morning, she was alone, but the light had been turned out, so she supposed he had found her asleep and gone to his own room.

It seemed like a portent of the future.

This morning, they had sat in their usual places, about as far apart as two people could be at the Blakes' big table. She had arranged that herself, how long ago? In the dark ages when she had believed she hated Jalal.

And now she loved him, but it was still a dark age....

"...probably a good idea to call," she surfaced to hear her mother saying.

He had smiled at her as he left with her father for the

marina a few minutes ago, but his smile, too, was dark with torment.

She thought of Zara, making the choice so easily, as if it were nothing more than a new dress—a new country, a new people, a new family…how could she have faced it so easily?

"Clio, where on earth are you this morning?"

"What?" She blinked, trying to replay the mental tape of what her mother had said, but she had been too deeply lost in her own thoughts even to record it. "Sorry, Mom, what did you say?"

"What is it, Clio? You look as though a Bearwalker is after you."

A little choke of laughter escaped her, and then suddenly she was weeping. "Oh, Mom, I don't want to leave here! I don't want to spend the rest of my life in a place where no one understands what a Bearwalker is!"

Maddy Blake jumped to her feet. "What? Darling, why should you? Leave?" Then her face lost all expression. "No!" she breathed. "Not Jalal? Not you and Jalal?"

"He asked me to marry him last night."

"Oh, darling! Not you, too! Oh, Lord, why didn't I listen when you said not to let him come? Oh, no, not you, too, thousands of miles away! Oh, will all my daughters leave me?"

"Mom, I didn't say yes. I love him, but how can I leave here? I *know* this is my home! If it were somewhere like Quebec or something—but so far away?" She buried her face in her hands. "Tell me what to do!" she whispered.

Her mother slipped into the chair beside her, put an arm around her daughter's shoulders.

"I wish I could just say, no I can't do it, and that would be the end of it. Why does love have to be so hard? I thought it was supposed to be wonderful—we didn't even get one day of real…real happiness.''

Her mother blew out a troubled breath. ''What a fool I was. Bring a man like him here…''

''What do you think, Mom? Could I be happy? Would I learn to love the country, would loving him make up for…everything?''

Maddy's eyes fell. ''I don't know, Clio,'' she said. She took a deep breath and tried to forget her own feelings. ''Don't forget, you'd have Zara close by. You wouldn't be…''

''Zara is in East Barakat. Jalal told me last night that his place is in the capital. That's miles away from Zara.''

The ice cream shop doorbell rang, and both women, instinctively responding to duty, looked up. ''That must be Willa with the ice cream,'' said Maddy.

''I'll go.'' Clio got up and bent to kiss her mother's cheek before dashing out to open the shop door for the delivery woman.

''Oh, boy, what a day that was!'' said Willa cheerfully. ''All that rain totally ruined my schedule!'' Willa was practically a one-woman band, making and delivering her ice cream, and even growing some of the fruit she used in it.

She and Clio had been friendly for years, just another of the pleasant strands of Clio's life that bound her here to Love Lake. She wasn't a close friend. If Clio moved to Barakat Willa was one of the many people she would probably never see again. A single thread in the tapestry of her life, perhaps, but still there would be a hole if it were plucked out.

''You feeling okay?'' Willa asked, as the two women unloaded the tubs of ice cream and carried them into the freezer.

"Yeah, just fine," Clio lied. "I had a bit of a headache yesterday, but it's going now."

A few minutes later she waved goodbye to Willa and began to prepare the shop for opening.

She stood for a moment looking around the shop. She had never wanted more than this. Zara had always had her ears tuned to a different drummer, but not Clio. She had never wanted a palace, she scarcely even hankered after one of the mansions on the lake. A few years ago her father had taken a vote on whether they wanted him to buy one of the big places that had come up for sale…they had all, in the end, preferred to stay where they were.

Wife of the Grand Vizier of the Barakat Emirates.

Arwen came in. "Gosh, what a fabulous day!" She suddenly looked at Clio. "Clio, what's the matter?"

"Nothing. I had a headache yesterday. I didn't sleep very well."

Arwen stood straight. "I can look after the shop if you want to go and take a swim or something."

"Thanks, honey, but there's actually quite a bit to do. The ice cream only came in this morning and we have to get all the tubs changed."

"Oh, boy, does the butter pecan need to be scraped out? Can I do it?"

The small joy of a sister who loved butter pecan ice cream. Clio stood looking at Arwen and knew that, one way or the other, this decision was going to kill her.

Eighteen

They made love that night with a passion that took them both to a country of wildest pleasure, and beyond its borders to a place of naked pain. To reach together that place of total union was to know that they were not truly united, and that night she wept with joy and sorrow intermingled.

Afterwards, they lay entangled in each other's arms, their bodies wet with their exertions in the hot night.

They chatted of uncontroversial things, like ordinary lovers, but in the back of her mind worry nibbled like a mouse at the cheese of her happiness.

"You said—" she began suddenly, almost without meaning to, then pressed her lips together and heaved a sigh. "Jalal, last night you said there was danger."

He nodded. "You wish me to tell you about it?"

"I think I have to know."

He paused, as if searching for the words. "There are

men who wish to overthrow the reign of my uncles. They wish to reunite the Barakat Emirates into the Kingdom of Barakat, under one king. A puppet king, whom they will control because they have put him in power.''

Her horrified breath hissed in her throat.

"You?"

His chin moved. ''I am of inestimable value to such a conspiracy. Because my father was Aziz, there are many in the country who believe, or will be convinced, that I have a valid right to the throne. And if these people are taught that the division of the kingdom has been a bad thing, if they are brought to anger because their frivolous rulers have all married foreign women—then they will accept it when they are told that the answer is to put another king on the old throne....''

"Is all this propagandizing going on now?" she asked.

"There are rumours, articles in certain papers. My uncles knew—suspected that it was not chance. But how to find those who instigate the unrest?

"So publicly they sent me abroad to study...but the rumour escaped that I had been banished for conspiring against them.''

In the warm night air, Clio suddenly began to shiver. She leaned over Jalal to pluck her nightshirt from the floor, then sat up cross-legged on the bed, slipped her arms into the sleeves and wrapped it around her, her arms tight across her breasts.

"What do you mean? Is it—I don't understand.''

"They hoped that this would make those who plotted believe that I would be vulnerable to an approach.''

Clio drew in a trembling breath. "Oh, Jalal, you mean—you're part of their investigation?" And all at once she realized how stupid her suspicions of him had been. Born of paranoia and fear. He was not a man built for betrayal.

"What else?" he said matter-of-factly, and she bit her lip in self-condemnation.

"But how dangerous! What if someone finds out you're playing a double game!"

He stroked her strong smooth thigh with a lazy hand. "That is why you must not speak of this to anyone. Now you have my life in your hands twice over."

She wished her heart would calm down. What a lousy conspirator she would make—her heart rate would give her away every time.

"Go on," she said.

"My uncles were right. I was approached."

"And—who is it?"

He shook his head. "Still I have no names. But last night they asked for another meeting. They have said they have something…they believe it will convince me to throw in with them."

"Do you mean they might think they have something they could blackmail you with?"

He shook his head helplessly. "It seems obvious, but I cannot imagine what this could be. The evil I have done is a matter of public record. Everyone knows I kidnapped Princess Zara. What else is there?"

Jalal shrugged. "So, they will show me this—whatever it is. If they also reveal who is their ringleader, as we hope, my job is done. But if not—I have discovered nothing, Clio! I have not learned anything of real value. And it may be impossible for me to go along with them any further. I may be faced with a choice that…something to which I must say no. And then it will be all for nothing."

She was frightened suddenly, shivering with nerves. "When is the meeting?"

"Tomorrow. It is possible that afterwards I will have to return to the Emirates." He paused, stroking her head, and her hair all down her back. "Clio, beloved, I ask you again to go with me."

She dropped her head in helpless misery. "Jalal, you don't know what you're asking. You told me once that you aren't at home anywhere. I am at home. This is my home. Please don't ask me to go to the desert to spend my life, when you yourself don't even feel it's home. Please don't."

"I should not have said this. Of course it is my home."

"But what would I *do* there?"

He said, "We could spend every summer here. In Barakat everyone who can leaves the city for the summer. We can do the same."

She tried to think of it as a solution that would make her happy.

"What would I do the other nine months of the year? Be your wife at social events?"

"And be a mother to our children."

"And what of our children—what if we have a son?" she demanded.

He arched up to kiss her. "I hope we have many sons."

She turned and looked down at him lying against her pillows in the soft pool of light. Was light ever so sweetly gentle in the desert?

"To provide more temptation for future conspirators?" she suggested. "This is an endless thing, isn't it? There will always be someone, won't there, looking for a figurehead, a puppet, to front for their ambitions? I don't want that for my children."

"People forget," he murmured half-heartedly, not wishing to see the truth of what she said. "They will forget I was anything but Grand Vizier."

"And that's another thing. I couldn't be a political wife, Jalal. I couldn't learn to take it all seriously, all that...I mean, Zara enjoys it. And anyway, she has a career. She's an archaeologist. Whether she's on a dig or building a museum, she takes that part of her with her.

"But that part of me is just what I can't take with me. For me that's the ice cream shop, it's working with my mother, it's all the little things. It's having home and work so smoothly entangled it's practically seamless.

"Why don't you stay here? You like it here, you said it's in your blood."

He shook his head, as she knew he would, and her heart clenched with pain. She could foresee no unblemished happiness for herself now.

She said miserably, "You know—Zara avoided getting serious with Peter Clifford, because he was a small-town guy, with small-town ambitions. She knew if she got involved with him, one of them would be unhappy. I didn't have that problem with Peter—his lifestyle would have suited me down to the ground. That was exactly the kind of marriage I wanted."

"I am sorry I am not this man," Jalal said stiffly.

"I'm sorry, I'm not explaining it well, but don't you see what I'm saying? Zara avoided getting mixed up with anyone who couldn't understand what sort of a future she had in mind, or wouldn't want to share it. And I—I tried to do the same.

"Only you came here, and—oh, it's not fair!" she cried. "I didn't ask for this! I didn't ask for a foreign prince to come here and sweep me off my feet!"

Out of the torment of indecision and anguish, she wept, but for once he did not understand. His own pain was too powerful in him. To love at last, to understand the great mystery of the other half—and to be rejected in this way…it was one rejection too many in his life.

Jalal stood up, pulled on his clothes. "The foreign prince will go away again," he said.

She suddenly understood that she had hurt him. "Why can't you understand?" she cried. "Why should it automatically be me who gives everything up? Why can't you move here? Why do you think I should just jump at giving up everything I ever wanted, and you don't even have to look at the possibility?"

"What will I do in this country? My home is Barakat," Jalal said with stiff formality. "Let me advise you to go to your first lover Peter and invite him into your bed again. After one hour with you he will forget he ever knew your sister's name. Then you will have everything you want."

"I do not love Peter Clifford, I love you!" she said stonily, not sounding at all like a woman who meant love.

"But somehow you do not stop dreaming of him."

He opened the door and went out. She let him go.

Saifuddin ar Ratib lifted a briefcase onto the table. "You asked," he began, "for some proof that my principals have sufficient influence to carry their plans into successful action."

"I also asked," Jalal put in dryly, "for some evidence as to who they are."

"The time is not yet ripe for that, but the evidence I bring you will show you how close to the heart of the monarchy and the reins of power my principal has always been."

He removed a file folder from the case, snapped it shut and set it to one side. He sat with the file under his hands for a moment, regarding Jalal thoughtfully. Then, pushing the entire folder across the table to him, he said softly, "Read this."

Jalal smiled at the neat orchestration of the moment. His appetite whetted, of course he was now expected to grab it open. He leaned back casually in his chair, his legs spread, so that The Arranger should detect no impatience in him, find no weak spot of eagerness, and threaded his fingers together over his stomach.

"And what is this that you would have me read?" He indicated the folder with an arrogant tilt of his nose. "Tell me why it should interest me."

"Merely some documents that you will find enlightening as to my principal's long-term intentions and convictions, and his ability to put his plans into action."

"I will need more than a sheaf of documentation to convince me that he can successfully overthrow the present monarchy and reinstate a unified Barakat."

The Arranger smiled. "Nevertheless, he believes you will find these papers of supreme interest."

Still in no hurry, Jalal nodded and sipped his mint tea. At last he reached a lazy hand for the folder.

The first thing that met his eyes was his own signature. "Jalal ibn Aziz ibn Daud al Quraishi." He flicked a glance at Saifuddin and then his eyes fell irresistibly back to the document. He frowned.

"I am Jalal, the son of your brother, Prince Aziz. You know my history. I now request the right to take my place…"

Jalal murmured the words aloud as the tendrils of memory reached out to claim him. He remembered the shape of the pen in his hands, the smell of his mother's cooking, remembered even the hot wind that had blown through the garden as he sat composing this first letter to his uncles, long years ago.

He looked up. "This is no more than the letter all the world knows I have written, to my uncles."

Saifuddin ar Ratib watched him steadily. "Note that it is the original letter," he said.

Jalal stroked the paper between finger and thumb, felt the tell-tale ridging. "How did you get this?"

The Arranger merely smiled and shook his head, lifting a casual finger to encourage Jalal to read on.

He turned to the next document.

"From Jalal ibn Aziz ibn Daud to his uncles the Princes: I am astonished to have received no reply to my letter…"

He was surprised, now, to see how clearly he had set out his parentage. Over time he had forgotten. How could his uncles have pretended, after reading these, that they did not know of his existence?

"From Jalal ibn Aziz…why do you call me grandson of a bandit? Was King Daud a bandit? Are his sons?"

And yet they had seemed so convincing when they at last understood and accepted him….

Was this how these people intended to convince him to commit himself? By proving that his uncles had lied and betrayed him from the beginning?

"From Jalal ibn Aziz to his uncles who ignore their father's deathbed behest, know that I am determined…"

He looked at the letters, both sides. "There is no palace stamp on any," he said, frowning.

With a stroke like lightning through his brain, he understood. His eyes lifted to meet the steady, assessing gaze of Saifuddin ar Ratib. Jalal struggled to control his emotions. He must allow this man no window onto his soul.

"My uncles never received these letters," he said slowly.

Saifuddin ar Ratib inclined his head in acknowledgement of the truth of this.

"That is the reason they did not know who I was. How was it done?" Jalal asked, struggling to maintain an appearance of calm. "How was it effected? My own letters were intercepted, and others substituted as if from me, omitting all mention of my claim to my birthright? A letter from Jalal the grandson of Selim, demanding land only because his grandfather had been a bandit with de facto ownership of the desert...."

He faded into silence, thinking of those months in which he had believed himself spurned by his family, his father's half brothers, feeling again the anguish and its transmogrification into fury.

"That is how you were presented to the princes, yes."

His eyes dropped back to the file. There were many more documents than these letters. He turned to the next.

A photocopy of an assessment from a commanding officer during his military training, the name of the recipient obliterated with the censor's wide black stroke, but the terms of respect in the body of the letter making it clear he wrote to someone with position in the palace, to whom he described Jalal's abilities and progress....

Half a dozen similar letters, charting his progress in the military. Then his graduating marks from university. Respectful letters to an unknown recipient describing various details and incidents of his university career. *"In extracurricular activities, too, he excels, his particular interests self-defence and swimming...."*

Letters from his schoolteachers, even. Everything.

His entire life, from the moment his mother, alone and desperate, had approached the palace, till he had returned to the desert and set up his camp. All here. All fully documented.

All that was missing were the letters he had sent after he abducted Zara.

"They never knew," Jalal said slowly, staring into the distant past. "My grandfather King Daud never knew of my existence. My grandmother…no one knew."

The dark head was graciously inclined. "That is true."

"My mother never learned the identity of the man she spoke to the day she went to the palace to reveal my existence. My uncles guessed that it was the late Nizam al Mulk, then the king's Grand Vizier. It was not Nizam al Mulk."

"It was not."

"It was not, as my mother believed, at the king's bidding that we moved to the city, that I was educated, that I was sent into officer training. It was this man. The man you call your principal."

The Arranger nodded. "May I say I admire the quickness of your grasp of the situation."

Jalal flicked him a look.

"What could his purpose have been in so great a deception lasting so many years? Revenge on my grandfather for some slight? Disdain for the illegitimacy of my birth?"

Saifuddin ar Ratib smiled. "Nothing so petty. He is a man of infinite patience and far-reaching command. When your mother arrived at the palace to tell her story, he saw at once the potential that might lie in your existence. The future he envisaged then for you required you to be carefully prepared, and he undertook to provide that preparation."

He sat as if listening to a distant voice.

"The preparation to be an outcast," Jalal murmured. "A man without roots. He tore me from the desert, from every subsequent certainty. All my life my mother spoke to me of a future different from what I was living…and that future never arrived. He knew my mother would break her silence eventually. It did not matter when. And when I made my representations to my uncles, he prevented their knowing me, as the final step in making me a rebel, the more easily to manipulate me," he added.

Saifuddin inclined his head. "You surprised him, however. Let it comfort you that he did not expect your return to the desert, nor the setting up of your camp. Nor the successful taking of a hostage, and forcing your uncles to recognize…"

Jalal showed his teeth. "You neither comfort me nor disturb my comfort with anything that you can say," he said with level contempt.

"And this fool—" he indicated the file with a flick of his hands and tossed it onto the table "—who has spent his life with this nonsense! Is such a man to be respected? This is not a fairy tale of lost heirs!"

He got to his feet. "Was it your intention to convince me that this man is a worthy partner in my endeavours? He is no more than a daydreaming old man. He mistakes plots for deeds," said Prince Jalal ibn Aziz ibn Daud al Quraishi, and he turned and went with contemptuous ease down the steps of the terrace to his boat.

Nineteen

The light shone under her door, showing that she was awake, and perhaps waiting for him.

Jalal knocked, and at her murmur, entered. She was sitting propped up by her pillows under a thin sheet, a magazine neglected in her lap.

"I heard your boat," she said. "Have you found out anything?"

"Yes." He came and sat on the bed. "He has exposed himself without realizing it. If I were not in contact with my uncles, there would be little risk to him in letting me know what I learned tonight. But my uncles will be able to guess, from what I tell them, who was in a position to do the things that he has done."

"So it's all over?"

"As to that—yes, one way or another, he is finished. Though it may take time to discover the full extent of the conspiracy."

She was silent, looking gravely into his eyes. "Then what is the bad news? What has so distressed you to-night?"

He stared at her. "How do you know it?"

She leaned close and smiled into his dark eyes. "You told me. When you came up the stairs I could hear it in your footsteps. I see it now, in your face."

His hand cupped her head, holding her there. His eyes searched her face for a moment.

"It is said in the stories that even so did my grand-mother understand my grandfather…without words. And he could read her mind also. My uncles say this is no more than the truth.

"They knew my grandfather and grandmother inti-mately, as father and beloved stepmother…I knew them only as king and queen of the country."

"Yes," she murmured sadly.

"This was always a mystery to me. From the moment I learned my true birthright I struggled to understand why my grandfather and grandmother had never wished to see me. You, too, said it. The son of their own beloved son. The single product of their great love. Yet they were sat-isfied to educate me from a distance. Why? My grandfa-ther lived more than a dozen years after my existence and parentage were discovered to him…so many days and years when we could have enjoyed each other's com-pany."

"He was an old man," she whispered.

"Something like this I have always told myself. I made many excuses for them—that the pain of meeting me would revive their old grief in the loss of their only sons. That my grandfather perhaps did not entirely believe my mother—her case could not then be proved, as it is now, with DNA tests. Or that the stain of my birth was an impossible barrier.

"Or perhaps he did not want to be faced with the choice of disinheriting his three younger sons or dividing the kingdom into four.... I told myself he avoided being tempted into these things by never meeting me, never loving me."

He paused, and she sat with him in silence and soft lamplight, waiting for his thoughts to form. Outside the soft circle of light, the world was dark and still. The water brushed the shore, a boat squeaked against a dock, wind murmured in the branches.

When he shook his head and heaved a breath, she reached both hands to clasp his head. "And what have you learned tonight that changes all that?" she asked gently.

"They never knew of my existence," he told her baldly. "My grandfather, my grandmother—they were robbed of the knowledge that one of their dead sons had left a son behind him. That is why they never summoned me to the palace. They did not know I was alive in the world. They died without knowing."

His pain was palpable in the room. Her heart clenched with sorrowing feeling.

"Oh, Jalal!" Clio whispered. "But then—your education, your whole life...who did they think you were when they did all that?"

"They knew nothing of these things. I have been, from the moment my mother went to the palace, a toy...a pawn in the hands of a man, a despicable man...."

"What?" she breathed, horrified.

Absently he stroked the delicate, precious line of her collarbone. "This man pretended to my mother that he told the king her secret. He acted as if on the king's orders, and passed on 'his' messages and instructions.''

''But why didn't she insist on your meeting your own grandparents?''

He shook his head at her. ''No, Clio, you do not understand—what did she know? She was an ignorant woman from the desert. She could not read. She had committed a grave sin with her princely lover, which she had to confess in order to tell the king of my existence. What could she understand of her value to the king? Or of mine? How could she insist that her illegitimate son meet his grandfather?''

''But even so—''

He touched her lips.

''Clio, you cannot understand such a woman as my mother. It is so far from anything you know. You are a free woman, knowing your importance in the world. Your father values you, your mother is a woman of influence, and you hope to be like her. You are the equal of your brothers. Even this ugliness with this man, Peter—he was one man who made you feel of less value than your sister. My mother has struggled against the opinion of all society, for the simple belief that she is a human being with value in God's eyes!''

His voice was choked with feeling. She made no reply, but waited for him to say what he needed to say.

''She was deeply and always grateful to her father—to her own father, Clio!—because he did not kill her and me with her in the womb! He did not deliver her to the tribe for stoning, but instead gave her into slavery with an old husband—when she had been the beloved of a prince!''

She whispered his name.

''When this man in the palace told her the king would never see her, but would support her and her son...this

was much more than in her heart she expected. Can you
see the huge bravery that she had, to go to the palace at
all? And there to insist on seeing someone of importance!
Perhaps the king would kill her for bearing his illegitimate
grandson. Perhaps she would be accused of lies, of trick-
ery…. How was she to know?

"The Prophet said, 'Women are the twin-halves of
men,' Clio, but he spoke to an ignorant desert people who
lived by the sword, who valued nothing but a man's sword
arm, and who would not learn the lesson. And still we go
on refusing to learn it, turning our backs on what he said,
the knowledge he brought fourteen hundred years ago.

He turned to her, lifting his hands to her face. Strong,
sure, they cupped her head, and he stared deep into her
dark eyes.

"They told me all this tonight for a purpose. They said
it was to convince me that the man behind all this is
powerful and can deliver on his promise. Close enough to
the throne to… But I know that it was psychological ma-
nipulation—they wanted to deliver such a blow at last
that, doubting everything, I would commit myself to them
finally and completely."

"And—did it work?"

"It has shaken me to my soul to know that my life is
so different from what I believed. To think that I have
been a pawn—deliberately frustrated so that my anger
could be used by this man for his own purposes. He created such an existence for me so that I would hate, because hatred can be twisted into useful shapes. And he
thought to make me a weapon in his own hands."

"Oh Jalal, what a monster he must be!" she said, feeling deeply helpless. What could be said to comfort such
appalling pain?

"Yes, a monster." He lifted a hand. "And a fool. A

fool. To spend twenty-five years on a plan that has no end, no goal, but destruction. Destruction of my uncles, of the whole structure of the Emirates…not one positive, one good, to anyone, nothing but backward ignorance and evil.

"And as long as I am in Barakat, Clio, I will be a focus for such madmen. Always I will be the nearest puppet prince for fools who cannot remember that the Prophet said also that a state survives without religion, but not without justice."

"*Did* he?" she interjected, amazed.

"Yes, and many other wise things that fools ignore."

He heaved a sigh and held her head between his hands. "You were right. How can I take you to that, to such a life of politics and conspiracy as would always surround us and our children?"

She was silent, breathless with hope, with shock, with love, with compassion.

"I have no life there now. Everything is severed. I am free from what I believed, from all that I wanted and fought for—free from the burden of my past and my history.

"If you accept me as your husband, Clio, I will stay here with you, and build a life amongst the lakes and forest. I will see that my grandmother's descendants return to the kind of land she loved, and our children will inherit what we build for them, and nothing more.

"Do you accept, my beloved? Will this please you as it pleases me?"

She was weeping too hard to answer.

In the King's Pavilion, four men lounged around the fountain, drinking mint tea, eating the rich powdered sweetmeats that lay on small silver trays.

"As long as I remain here, how can I fail to be a focus for every sect that is disenchanted with the state of the monarchy or the country?" Jalal asked. "It's too obvious, too easy. I don't want to spend my life being tempted, by one manipulator after another, to overthrow your joint rule, against my grandfather's clear wishes."

"Father might have had other wishes, if he had been privileged to know of your existence," Omar said. "It's possible that you would even have been seen as a way out of his dilemma. He could have favoured you over all three of us, with the country's blessing, and none of his wives could have complained. And the kingdom would have remained undivided."

Jalal nodded. It was true. Perhaps it would always remain a tormenting mystery, what course his life would have followed if Selim had taken his pregnant daughter immediately to the palace, instead of playing a deeper game, or if, when his mother at last went, she had not fallen into ambitious hands....

At the very least, perhaps, his uncles would have seemed like cousins, or brothers, rather than the virtual strangers they now were. And he might have felt at home in his father's grand palace.

"Perhaps. In that case, however, I would have been raised to the task of rule. But I was not. You were, and you do it well. All of you." He looked around. "The people love you, and they love your beautiful, foreign wives. If I am not here to be always pointed to as an alternative...the little discontents will seep into the ground and be lost."

"What are you saying, Jalal?" Rafi asked.

Rafi's near twin set down the tiny gold-etched teacup, and waited till the eyes of all three princes were on him.

"I want to leave Barakat. I will renounce my father's titles and go abroad to live. I want to be done with the quest for power and recognition, and for family."

There was silence as they took it in, each in his own particular way. Omar gazed absently at the sparkling fountain, stroking his beard, listening intently; Karim raised his eyebrows, nodding; Rafi looked at his all-but-twin with a level, assessing gaze.

The silence stretched and stretched.

"Where will you go?" Karim asked.

And Rafi suggested softly, "Clio?"

Jalal's head bent in a quick nod. "Yes, Clio. I will buy a house on a lake where she has lived all her life. I have spoken to her father about the business. We think of me investing in it, perhaps…or I would like to invest in water purification, industrial waste treatment, to keep the lakes free from pollution."

"Jalal, are you sure about all this?"

Jalal ibn Aziz ibn Daud ibn Hassan al Quraishi nodded. "Yes, I am sure," he said. "Sure."

The old church at Love's Point had not seen such a crowd for a very long time. The congregation glowed as they spilled into the quiet, tree-lined streets, everyone dressed in the most beautiful outfits in their wardrobe, young and old, rich and poor, prince and commoner alike.

The marriage between Clio Blake and Jalal al Quraishi had taken place in the 150-year-old church, and the reception had followed in the beautiful gardens, with their flowered lawns rolling down to the banks of the quiet, pretty river.

The bride was beautiful in traditional white, her elegant, long-sleeved matte satin dress smoothly fitted from breast to hip, and billowing into folds down to her feet, her train as gauzy and romantic over her long flowing hair as any of her young bridesmaids could have wished.

They all wore white, with tiny seed pearl and flower wreaths in their hair, and as they crowded around Clio now, they looked like vestal virgins accompanying their goddess.

In the street a white limousine, now sporting a massive Just Married sign and strings trailing numerous tin cans, bore witness to the labours of some among the congregation during the past hour. A long line of cars behind proved that many of the guests intended to accompany the bridal couple on the first leg of their journey, to the airport, where they would board a flight for an unknown destination.

The late-September sun was smiling and warm as the congregation stood in happy groups, and a small breeze obligingly lifted the bride's veil and blew it picturesquely around her.

There were still pictures being taken, but these were all by friends, the media long since having taken their photos of the bride and groom, as well as Prince Rafi and the prettily pregnant Princess Zara of East Barakat, and departed to meet their deadlines.

Everyone stood around chatting, unwilling to leave, or bring an end to a lovely day. The bride and groom stood in the church path smiling and talking to well-wishers, until someone looked at his watch and said, "Well, time to get started, if you want to catch that plane."

Clio and Jalal smiled wickedly into each other's eyes, and then clasped each other's hand and started...not towards the car, but along the curving paved pathway that led down under willow trees to the river.

They turned back, giving the startled congregation one

last chance for a photo, smiled and waved, and then set off lightly running down to the river.

Before anyone could seriously get it together to realize what was going on, they were seen climbing into a large powerboat that was moored by the bank, and by the time anyone had arrived at the river, the engine was running smoothly and the groom was guiding the boat out into the narrow river.

"Bye!" they called, laughing as the congregation spilled down the banks and, mouths open with smiling surprise, stood waving at the disappearing couple, Clio standing within the embrace of Jalal's arm as he drove, her veil streaming wildly out behind.

After a moment they were out of sight, under the bridge, heading out into the lake.

Clio unpinned her veil and tossed it lightly down into the cabin, then shook her long hair and stretched luxuriously up towards the sun, tilting her head to smile at her new husband.

"Hello," she said softly.

He flicked a glance around for any approaching boat, and seeing none, took his eyes off the water long enough to cup her head in one powerful hand and kiss her willing mouth with contained passion.

"Hello," he said, with proud possessiveness.

"Oh, what a beautiful day!" she exclaimed, happiness shimmering through her voice. "Wasn't it fabulous?"

"Fabulous," he agreed, with a look at her that melted her so that she had to close her eyes.

"Do you think they'll guess where we're going?"

"Maybe. Your friends maybe. But let's hope they won't tell anyone who really wants to know."

"Maybe the press will be happy with pictures of Zara and Rafi for the next week."

"We don't have to worry. Today they want our photographs, but we will soon be very ordinary people."

She kissed him. "Yes, to think I could have married a prince!" She lifted a haughty shoulder. "I'll always be able to tell our children that a prince once proposed to me!"

"And I will always be able to tell them that you turned the prince down for a commoner," he said.

They took the familiar route, across the lake, through a channel, into another lake, and at last making their way up Bent Needle River towards Solitaire. A few minutes later the boat drew up by the dock, and Clio stepped out, still in her gracefully beautiful dress, with the bow line.

She stood on the dock in the late sun while Jalal made the boat fast, sighing in happiness as she took in the rich reds and yellows of the turning leaves. And then they caught each other's hand again and started up the path to their honeymoon cottage and a new life.

* * * * *

SILHOUETTE'S 20TH ANNIVERSARY CONTEST
OFFICIAL RULES
NO PURCHASE NECESSARY TO ENTER

1. To enter, follow directions published in the offer to which you are responding. Contest begins 1/1/00 and ends on 8/24/00 (the "Promotion Period"). Method of entry may vary. Mailed entries must be postmarked by 8/24/00, and received by 8/31/00.

2. During the Promotion Period, the Contest may be presented via the Internet. Entry via the Internet may be restricted to residents of certain geographic areas that are disclosed on the Web site. To enter via the Internet, if you are a resident of a geographic area in which Internet entry is permissible, follow the directions displayed on-line, including typing your essay of 100 words or fewer telling us "Where In The World Your Love Will Come Alive." On-line entries must be received by 11:59 p.m. Eastern Standard time on 8/24/00. Limit one e-mail entry per person, household and e-mail address per day, per presentation. If you are a resident of a geographic area in which entry via the Internet is permissible, you may, in lieu of submitting an entry on-line, enter by mail, by hand-printing your name, address, telephone number and contest number/name on an 8"x 11" plain piece of paper and telling us in 100 words or fewer "Where In The World Your Love Will Come Alive," and mailing via first-class mail to: Silhouette 20th Anniversary Contest, (in the U.S.) P.O. Box 9069, Buffalo, NY 14269-9069; (In Canada) P.O. Box 637, Fort Erie, Ontario, Canada L2A 5X3. Limit one 8"x 11" mailed entry per person, household and e-mail address per day. <u>On-line and/or 8"x 11" mailed entries received from persons residing in geographic areas in which Internet entry is not permissible will be disqualified.</u> No liability is assumed for lost, late, incomplete, inaccurate, nondelivered or misdirected mail, or misdirected e-mail, for technical, hardware or software failures of any kind, lost or unavailable network connection, or failed, incomplete, garbled or delayed computer transmission or any human error which may occur in the receipt or processing of the entries in the contest.

3. Essays will be judged by a panel of members of the Silhouette editorial and marketing staff based on the following criteria:

> Sincerity (believability, credibility)—50%
>
> Originality (freshness, creativity)—30%
>
> Aptness (appropriateness to contest ideas)—20%

Purchase or acceptance of a product offer does not improve your chances of winning. In the event of a tie, duplicate prizes will be awarded.

4. All entries become the property of Harlequin Enterprises Ltd., and will not be returned. Winner will be determined no later than 10/31/00 and will be notified by mail. Grand Prize winner will be required to sign and return Affidavit of Eligibility within 15 days of receipt of notification. Noncompliance within the time period may result in disqualification and an alternative winner may be selected. All municipal, provincial, federal, state and local laws and regulations apply. Contest open only to residents of the U.S. and Canada who are 18 years of age or older, and is void wherever prohibited by law. Internet entry is restricted solely to residents of those geographical areas in which Internet entry is permissible. Employees of Torstar Corp., their affiliates, agents and members of their immediate families are not eligible. Taxes on the prizes are the sole responsibility of winners. Entry and acceptance of any prize offered constitutes permission to use winner's name, photograph or other likeness for the purposes of advertising, trade and promotion on behalf of Torstar Corp. without further compensation to the winner, unless prohibited by law. Torstar Corp and D.L. Blair, Inc., their parents, affiliates and subsidiaries, are not responsible for errors in printing or electronic presentation of contest or entries. In the event of printing or other errors which may result in unintended prize values or duplication of prizes, all affected contest materials or entries shall be null and void. If for any reason the Internet portion of the contest is not capable of running as planned, including infection by computer virus, bugs, tampering, unauthorized intervention, fraud, technical failures, or any other causes beyond the control of Torstar Corp. which corrupt or affect the administration, secrecy, fairness, integrity or proper conduct of the contest, Torstar Corp. reserves the right, at its sole discretion, to disqualify any individual who tampers with the entry process and to cancel, terminate, modify or suspend the contest or the Internet portion thereof. In the event of a dispute regarding an on-line entry, the entry will be deemed submitted by the authorized holder of the e-mail account submitted at the time of entry. Authorized account holder is defined as the natural person who is assigned to an e-mail address by an Internet access provider, on-line service provider or other organization that is responsible for arranging e-mail address for the domain associated with the submitted e-mail address.

5. Prizes: Grand Prize—a $10,000 vacation to anywhere in the world. Travelers (at least one must be 18 years of age or older) or parent or guardian if one traveler is a minor, must sign and return a Release of Liability prior to departure. Travel must be completed by December 31, 2001, and is subject to space and accommodations availability. Two hundred (200) Second Prizes—a two-book limited edition autographed collector set from one of the Silhouette Anniversary authors: Nora Roberts, Diana Palmer, Linda Howard or Annette Broadrick (value $10.00 each set). All prizes are valued in U.S. dollars.

6. For a list of winners (available after 10/31/00), send a self-addressed, stamped envelope to: Harlequin Silhouette 20th Anniversary Winners, P.O. Box 4200, Blair, NE 68009-4200.

Contest sponsored by Torstar Corp., P.O. Box 9042, Buffalo, NY 14269-9042.

ENTER FOR
A CHANCE TO WIN*

Silhouette's 20th Anniversary Contest

Tell Us Where in the World
You Would Like *Your* Love To Come Alive...
And We'll Send the Lucky Winner There!

Silhouette wants to take you wherever
your happy ending can come true.

Here's how to enter: Tell us, in 100 words or less,
where you want to go to make your love come alive!

In addition to the grand prize, there will be 200
runner-up prizes, collector's-edition book sets
autographed by one of the Silhouette anniversary
authors: **Nora Roberts, Diana Palmer,
Linda Howard** or **Annette Broadrick**.

DON'T MISS YOUR CHANCE TO WIN!
ENTER NOW! No Purchase Necessary

Where love comes alive™

Visit Silhouette at www.eHarlequin.com to enter, starting this summer.

Name:

Address:

City: State/Province:

Zip/Postal Code:

Mail to Harlequin Books: **In the U.S.**: P.O. Box 9069, Buffalo, NY
14269-9069; **In Canada**: P.O. Box 637, Fort Erie, Ontario, L4A 5X3